CARROLL & GRAF

White Thighs

White Thighs

ANONYMOUS

Carroll & Graf Publishers, Inc.
New York

First Carroll & Graf edition 1986
Fourth printing 1991

Carroll & Graf Publishers, Inc.
260 Fifth Avenue
New York, NY 10001

ISBN: 0-88184-244-3

Manufactured in the United States of America

White Thighs

Madge Buford

My dear Jack:

I have just received your doleful letter and my heart and something else further down yearn to console you. But what can I do for you, way out there in a camp in the Rocky Mountains, with "not a cunt within a hundred miles" as you say?

Poor Jack, and you so amorous! Would that I had you here, naked in my arms, your ardent kisses covering me from lips to knees, your darling staff resting rigid in my grasp or receiving a caress from parted lips, until ready to burst with its creamy treasures, you would throw me on my back, and breast to breast, belly to belly, tongues hotly thrust into eager, suckling mouths, and arms and legs so interwoven that one could hardly tell—which you, which me—while that stiff staff of yours, that Cyprian sceptre of delight was plunged deeply in my belly. Those soul inspiring thrusts carried such a thrill of ecstasy to my eager cunt, until the acme of all human joy was reached and my thirsty womb drank in the balmy sweets of manly sperm and I bedewed you with my own full measure of ecstatic overflow!

Oh Jack! Dear Jack! would that you were here. But wishes are vain. A thousand miles are between us. But Jack! I remember that the last summer we were together at the seashore you often asked me to tell you of myself, to give you a history of my amorous life; and

I put it off until, at last, our pleasure-giving days were rudely cut short by that sudden order from the War Department to join your regiment.

And now, dear Jack! I've the thought that perhaps, while you're away so far, a few pages from my life might give you pleasure, even if the pleasure had to end like Onan's, in the Bible, and the seed be wasted on the barren, western soil, instead of thrilling this yearning crevice of mine that calls out so eagerly to you as I write.

CHAPTER I

I was born in Louisiana among the palms, pelicans, and bayous, where the soft air has an amorous embrace and the half-tropical sun breeds voluptuousness. When I was fourteen my father received a consular appointment in Europe and it was thought best that I should be left in America to complete my education. I can remember no relations of my parents except a middle-aged uncle of my mother's, Uncle John we called him, who was rich but a recluse; going now and then to New Orleans on business, when he would make a formal call, and burying himself at other times in his large plantation, which was isolated in a part of the state distant from any other town.

My parents finally settled on the Convent of the Sacred Heart, in New York, as the place at which I was to complete my education and, taking me there, left me in charge of the sisters, while they sailed for Europe.

I have read much of the illicit intercourse of priests and sisters and novices; but I can recall nothing in this Convent that would raise a blush, even though perhaps I was too young to understand things that, to my present mind, would be suggestive.

Two years passed quietly and in all innocence. I was daily expecting the return of my parents when, one morning, the New York journals were filled with accounts of a great ocean disaster and, in a few years, I knew that I was alone in the world. Not a living soul on earth to look after me, a girl of sixteen.

The good sisters consoled me and treated me with more kindness than ever; but the uncertainty of my future preyed on me and I knew not where to turn. One day, just before the end of the session, I was summoned to the office, and there, with outstretched hand, was Uncle John.

He always seemed so far apart from the rest of us that I had not thought of him. But now he was all kindness and soon made me understand that he was to be my protector and that, for the present at any rate, I was to go live with him at his home.

CHAPTER II

"Beauvoir," out of the world as it was, charmed me. A one story house buried among magnolias; a wide piazza all around it, with hammocks and luxurious couches, for here one lives out of doors.

Uncle John told me that the Negro quarters were an eighth of a mile away and that the darkies were not permitted near the house unless summoned. The household servants were Sam and Meg, husband and wife; light-colored mulattoes, showing the Caucasian features of some white ancestor and each with a form and bearing that would fascinate a sculptor.

I was made at home in a pretty room and Meg assisted me in changing my traveling clothes and robing me in thin garments that left arms and neck bare; meanwhile the kind girl praised my shape and budding charms and I, in turn, laughingly lauded her well-developed figure; making her lift her plump breasts out of her dress and even raise her skirts so that I might see as much of her as she had of me; and so, half naked, I embraced her. For the first time in my life a new sensation seized me, and I know now that voluptuousness was at that moment born within me.

But supper was ready and I, seated opposite Uncle John, ate ravenously and drank some wine, a new thing for me which seemed to add to that unknown sensation that still lingered from Meg's embrace. After supper Uncle John showed me over the house, even to his luxurious bedroom, which was some distance from mine; and then, as I had had a long trip, he called Meg and said that I had better go to bed.

I kissed him, and again that tingling of unknown desires came to me as he pressed me to him; but I was not so overcome that I did not hear him whisper to Meg to come to him as soon as I was in bed. It did not take long with her help, and, wishing me pleasant dreams, she left. I lay in the dark, nervous, unsatisfied; wanting something, I knew not what.

I tried to analyze my feelings; find what it was that ailed me; felt of myself to see where the sensation came from. As my roving hand passed over the rounded belly to the tufted mount below, it touched the swelling sentinel of love and my thrilling nerves told me that *here* is what I sought. Feeling the soft crevice, I found, in my gently moving hand, a giver of unknown pleasures, until, my desires teaching my virgin instincts, I threw off the bedclothes, pulled up my night robe, opened wide my legs and, pressing my finger between my cunt's hot lips, soon learned the exquisite delight of rapid friction and lay dissolved in a gulf of languorous pleasure whose meaning I had not yet fathomed. What could it be? My hand and hairy mount were wet with some sticky exudation; my heart beat queerly and I lay in a delicious languour.

I could not make it out and again sought the mysterious grotto, but it did not feel nice, sticky as it was, and I got up and bathed myself. Refreshed, I was about to step into bed when the closing of a door at the other end of the hall made me pause. I heard Uncle John whisper to Meg to come to his room. What for? Could it be anything connected with the delightful phenomena I had just experienced myself? Instinct—the Devil—or I know not what, put it into my virgin mind that it was.

CHAPTER III

The newborn lust within me drove me on. Opening the door I stepped into the dark corridor and there, from the open ventilators over the closed door, a bright light shone, a beacon guiding me to a new revelation.

Soon I was close to it and could hear Meg and Uncle John talking; words which I hardly knew the meaning of. I was on pins and needles. A high backed chair stood near. Bracing it against the side of the door I climbed up on its back and my head came to a level with the open panel; the whole, brightly lighted room was in full view. Room? Think you I saw aught of it? No! For, there on the sofa, naked as Adam, sat Uncle John, leaning back, one hand holding the cigar he was smoking, the other the erect standard of love. For the first time I saw the maker of us all, the emblem of fertility; the one thing on earth without which a woman would be a useless creation and her teeming, yearning womb a sterile desert.

Oh, how my eyes glued themselves to his darling object! How my itching crevice told my innocence that this was what it yearned for. A column, white as alabaster, long and rigid, crowned as it were, with a jaunty red cap rolling down at the sides like the barbs of an arrow; and, at the other end, a great bag as large as my fist and rosy red; while all around this lovely machinery of love, black hair curled in close ringlets, forming a dark background against which the ivory sceptre stood out rampant, the true and only insignia of love.

"Strip, you minx," he said. "I've a whole bag full of sperm for you." And Meg, erect before him, almost with a turn of her hand, stood out in her olive nakedness. Plump arms and legs rounded gracefully; breasts that were veritable tents of love, and swelling belly that seemed to say, "Come press me." "Are you glad to have him back, Meg?" said Uncle John. For all response the darling girl threw herself back on her knees between him, and taking the hairy bag in one hand, with the other she gently grasped the rigid spear moving the white skin up and down, as I could see; for one minute the spry head was covered, the next, exposed and ready to burst. Then the girl sprang to her feet, rushed to the bed and, on her back, her bottom on the edge and with thighs wide open, cried out: "Come, Master John, come quick! My cunt is on fire! Fuck me! Fuck my cunt!" In an instant I saw the great red head of his cock pressed into the thick curling hair between her legs and, as his hands seized her buttocks, lose itself completely in the fervid crevice.

Lost, yes, for an instant; then out it comes again almost to the head, then in, then out, faster and faster. "Oh, it's lovely!" cried Meg. "I'm spending, give it to me!" and, with a quick movement, the panting girl threw her legs around his waist as, with throbbing breasts and heaving belly, I could guess that something, I knew not what, was being shot from his hidden pego—for she cried out to him as she clutched him in the last frantic throes: "Give me every drop of it!"

I could stand no more; sliding down from the chair I groped my way back to my room and to bed and, in a frenzy of feverish lust, I frigged myself till I fell asleep, languid and exhausted.

CHAPTER IV

With all my lustful yearnings I was frightened at what I had seen and what I had done to myself. For two days I struggled to keep amatory thought out of my head and my hands away from the center of pleasure. But it was useless. Naked men and women danced before my eyes. I wandered out in the grounds where the poultry were picking their crops full and a stately rooster would make a dive, mount a squawking hen and, with flushed face and puckering slit, I watched their brief spasms of jerks until the cock dismounted and the hen went away shaking her feathers.

One day I was walking along the road and, in the field not fifty feet away from me, a cow was grazing placidly. Suddenly I heard a low bellowing and, across the field, I saw a bull jump the fence and, with a mad rush, make for the cow, who, seeing him coming, turned to run. But it was too late. With a wild rush the lustful animal sprang forward; for an instant I saw him raised on his hind legs, that monstrous instrument of his sticking out like a mast from his belly; then down he came upon the cow's back, his forelegs clutching her sides and his panting flanks working like the piston rod of a steam engine until, the discharge coming, his speed lessened and I felt sure that he was experiencing the same languor that I had felt the night I saw Uncle John and Meg together.

The sight fired me: I forgot my good resolutions and, rushing to a little clump of trees, I pulled up my skirts and with eager hand, rubbed the itching of my carnal cavity until the ecstasy of a copious discharge left me limp.

From that day to this I have not checked my amorous desires when a person and place suited, and prudery alone stood in the way.

That night, as Uncle John kissed me good-night, I saw his eyes sparkle as they looked down upon the blossoming bubbies which my frock but partly hid; the arms around my waist dropped down and, with a spasmodic motion, he pressed my buttocks until we were so close together that I thought that I felt a hard substance in his breeches print itself against my belly. An instant thus, and releasing me he hastened to his room and I to mine.

I was wild; I stripped to my chemise and, barefooted, stole along the hall, mounted my chair and, again, through the fanlight, saw the heaven I yearned for.

With gently frigging hands between my legs, I saw him undress until, naked, he stood there, his lovely cock bolt upright against his belly. He took it in his hand and, the better to see it, I made a movement on my perch and—well—the next I knew I was on my back on the floor.

CHAPTER V

There, half stunned, ashamed, I lay a moment and before I could collect myself and fly, the door opened wide, the light streamed full upon my almost naked person and Uncle John stood over me.

I simply covered my face with my hands and lay there panting. In an instant I was lifted in his strong arms, one around my naked waist and the other hand pressed to my hairy nest.

In an instant my chemise was torn away and I lay naked in his lap, his eyes burning into mine, his hands wandering from my firm globes over my swelling belly and nestling between my legs, and his fingers penetrating the lips of love. "So—so—Miss Madge, you wanted to see what a man looked like, did you? So you shall. Give yourself up to it, dear!"

His hot lips were pressed to mine, his tongue thrust hotly in and then my nipples were his prey and his rapture-giving hand soon brought my heaving thighs to a climax of enjoyment.

"Oh!" I cried, throwing my arms around his neck. "This is heaven!" "Yes, my dear girl, for you; but I'm in hell! Just see!" Lifting me up and standing by my side, he took my hand and carried it to his overwrought pego. Oh! the first touch of that velvety truncheon! The quick grasp!—and then, his hand guided mine in the rapid, electric moving of the flexible skin upon the fixed flesh beneath—his buttocks working, his arm clutching me closely to him! "Go on! Go on!" he cried. "Watch it Madge, watch it shoot!" I felt his prick swell larger and larger in my grasp; his lips poured ravishing kisses on every spot of flesh he could reach and then—high in the air flew great drops of thick milky sperm-drops coming so fast that they seemed to be a stream of love lava.

Slowly the spasm quieted, and seizing me in his arms, he threw me flat on the bed and rolled on top of me, breast to breast, belly to belly, open mouth to open mouth, breathing into each other; tongue sucking, each of his hands grasping a plump cheek of my buttocks and his fallen but lusty prick and balls rubbing against my sensitive cunt until, with a a convulsive clutch, with arms and legs around him, I poured down my oblation to the god of love.

As I lay languishing he seized my hand and put his stiffened pego in its grasp, asking me if I did not want to examine it, and, as I held it upright, moving the soft skin gently up and down or weighing in my hand the heavy bag of love elixer, he told me all about it—why it stiffened, how it broke its way into the virgin slit, and sowed the seeds from which we all grow. He told me of the danger of indiscreet commerce in this artificial and conventional world. But he told me also, the many ways that lustful pleasure could be had with perfect safety. His glowing language and gentle but hot caresses re-illuminated the fires within me and I pressed my ardent mount convulsively to his hand. "You want more do you?" he cried. "Yes, dear John, give me more. I'm hotter than ever!" Flat on his back, his head and shoulders raised on a pillow, he lifted me up, straddled me across him, and, pulling me towards his face kissed my navel, belly, and thighs. Then his hot lips sought my eager cunt; his tongue gently tickled the sensitive membrane until squirming and wriggling from its embraces, I gave a cry of pleasure. Thrusting his elongated tongue deep into my burning slit, he worked it in and out, holding me tightly to his face, until my whole body seemed to dissolve itself in a blissful overflow and go gushing down to meet his lascivious embraces.

He held me thus for a moment, weltering in my enjoyment, then seizing me, he laid me on my back against the pillows straddled across my chest—"Make a cunt of your titties," he cried, and as his proud prick pressed against my breasts, I squeezed my plump globes around it and held it tightly. His buttocks began to work and I had the lovely spectacle, close to my eyes, of his swelling staff, now all in view; then only its ruby head shining between my snowy bubbies—when, ready to spend, he cried: "Now watch it!" and the great jets of cloudy essence flew high over my head, hit my cheek, fell in a copious shower on shoulder, arm and breast until, seizing my head, he raised me up—"Suck it!" he cried. "Make a cunt of your mouth; squeeze my balls! That's it—roll your tongue around it! That's good—suck harder; swallow every drop I've got," until breathless, I threw myself back and he, springing up, brought my thighs to the edge of the bed. Kneeling, holding my buttocks firmly in his grasp, he brought down again my ever ready balm with lightning working tongue.

He would not let me stay longer, but bathing me with refreshing cologne, took me in his arms and carried me to bed, making me promise not to touch my touchy tid-bit, but go straight to sleep. But, before he left my bedside I threw my arms around his hips and rained a dozen kisses on the now fallen and flabby idol of my desires.

CHAPTER VI

The next day he told me how debilitating and injurious it was to yield to love too much, especially in one so young; but he promised me that, on the morrow, he would again taste pleasure.

The morrow came. He ordered the horses saddled and we had a bracing gallop through the woods, returning with blood pounding healthfully through our veins and ravenously hungry. We ate heartily and two glasses of old wine made my whole body tingle with voluptuous desires.

"How demure and modest you look in that riding habit," said he. "I don't feel so," I answered and, unbuttoning my waist with both hands, I held up to him my stiff-nippled titties. "How lovely!" he cried. "Now let me see the other hill, the shaded mount of Venus." And, jumping to my feet, I pulled the long, modest, black riding habit up to my waist and exposed to his ardent eyes my palpitating belly. He was on his feet in an instant, and tearing open his trousers pointed his darling dart lustfully at me across the table. "Fill your glass!" he cried. "Fill it full. Drink it all; you to this branch of coral—I, to that rosy crevice." Draining the glasses—the lively wine spread still more ardent fires in our veins.

"Run!" he cried. "Lift your clothes as high as they will go and run ahead of me to my room." And, snatching up my skirts I threw them over my shoulder and ran at full speed along the hall; throwing myself, panting, upon the bed and he on me. His stiff cock rubbed against my belly and against my hairy mount; then, turning me upon my stomach, he pressed it against my plump backsides and, as it nestled cosily between the rounded cheeks, he rubbed it there, while his eager hand sought out my raging slit, and cock and hand moving in unison, we both went off together in delightful ecstasy.

Recovering, we stripped and, making me stand on a sofa with one leg lifted on his arm, he washed away the sticky overflow, bathed me with perfume and, giving my mount a parting kiss, I jumped down and he took my place while I, in turn, bathed him and paid him back with kisses on his humble cock.

Going to a bookcase he brought out a volume, and taking me on his lap, he opened it. Oh, such pictures! Naked men and women coupled together in every conceivable way! All the forms and fashions of lust which the lecherous imagination of centuries have invented and practiced; what a revelation it was! My hand instinctively sought his prick while, with one arm under my bottom, his fingers stroked my pussy. Each page was new and provocative. We were nearing the need for action, when, skipping a number of pages, he opened to a picture of a lovely girl upon her side and a handsome man in front of her, his head buried between her thighs and her lustful mouth filled with his inflamed pego. "How splendid!" I cried. "Both can enjoy it at once," and springing up, I threw myself prone upon the soft crimson rug on the floor. In a moment he was beside me, his lips covering my burning slit, his tongue tickling and thrusting, while my eager mouth closed tightly on his lovely, ruby headed spear; kissing, tongue-rolling, bag squeezing, buttock clutching—sucking, till the thick sperm bathed our mouths, throats and was gulped down to seethe in lustful satisfaction in our bellies.

We lay ten minutes thus lost in delicious lassitude. Don't say that sucking the carnal parts is digusting! Why is not a prick or cunt as clean and wholesome to kiss and taste as a mouth? Why, if I will let a cock play tag in my belly, should I be squeamish if he wants to enjoy the contact of lips and tongue? Both openings are lined with the same membrane and one is as wholesome as the other.

Let the prude pucker only with her slit if she chooses; but for me my lover is welcome to all the holes I've got.

John filled a goblet with wine and, as I still lay panting on the floor, handed it to me and, drinking half, he finished it. Then, getting upon the bed, he filled it again and made me bring my buttocks to the edge of the bed, prop myself up on a pillow, stretch my thighs wide-open and round up my belly. He then poured the whole glassful down the crevice of my slit, his mouth catching it below and his lips and tongue licking up the last drops. Then, again filling the goblet, he gave it to me and, kneeling before me, I washed and bathed his fallen cunt tickler in the wine and then drank all of it—ending by kissing away the drops that hung from his staff or glistened on the curly hair or swollen testicles.

Then he went and got the picture book which we had not finished, and reclining against the pillows, he seated me between his thighs, his prick pressed against my bottom and my legs spread out between his.

Smutty pictures are the true arrows of Venus. Half the women in the world are awkward in attempting lust; backward in lewd variety even when they are willing and anxious to please. But they are imitative and a picture from life will give them a carnal wrinkle.

Turning over the leaves of this concupiscent gallery of lecherous attitudes we came to one which I did not understand. A woman lying belly down across the waist high arm of a sofa, her magnificent bum showing its sumptuous and luxurious richness of flesh in bold prominence; behind her a man had his long and slender staff embedded—where? Not in her slit; it's too far back for that. "What a poor drawing!" I said. "Her quim is not there, it's further front." John laughed. "Don't you know my dear, that every woman has two openings down there? That fellow has his prick in her cul: in plain English, in her ass-hole. It's tight and fits a cock snugly and some men lust for that more than for the regular channel. They even rut this way with young children, boys, or with other men."

"How funny," I said. "I never dreamed of such a thing." And as I spoke, John's stiffened prick stuck between the broad cheeks of my buttocks.

I looked up into his face. "Do you want to?" I asked. He did not answer, but, jumping up, thrust his pego into my face. "Wet it with your mouth," he cried, "so that it will slide easier." And I obeyed, spreading the saliva over end and sides, so that when he took it out, it glistened with moisture. Lifting me up he led me to the sofa and, pushing me over the cushioned arm, had my broad buttocks boldly offered to his attack. Quickly he penetrated my cul; slowly like a new glove the yielding sides made room for its rigid visitor. It smarted, but I did not wince. I clutched the sofa and braced myself to meet his new and bolder storming of my person. What was the smart to the novelty of these new sensations? And when, passing his hand in front, he fingered my clitoris, I cried out: "Don't mind me; put it in all the way. I don't mind the hurt," and with feelings wound up to the fullest tension of lustful activity by the novel scabbard in which his sword was sheathed, he urged it boldly in almost to the hilt. Keeping time with fucking cock and frigging hand, I soon felt the swelling forerunner of dissolving bliss and, with wanton, wriggling thighs, spent freely in his hand while my stretched cul received the easing balm of his discharge.

CHAPTER VII

Twice a week our naked bodies worshipped in the temple of Venus and Priapus. On other days we were so simply affectionate, like father and daughter; avoiding all provocation and storing up the amorous juices and energy that made us fresh and eager for our holiday of lasciviousness.

I often wondered if Meg and Sam knew what was going on. If they did they made no sign—and as John (I had dropped the Uncle after our first bare-bellied bout) said nothing about them I kept silent.

A rainy Sunday came. John and I had passed the morning in the library, he with a bundle of journals which had just arrived and I with a sentimental novel that made me yawn. Presently it was dinner time and chatting pleasantly, I noticed that John filled my glass with wine more freely than usual. Soon I felt its exciting effects, felt them most acutely down in that touchy little crevice that was palpitating under the tablecloth. But I had promised not to seek pleasure except on the regular days and I kept silent.

"Madge," he said, "this is my birthday."

"Oh! I wish I had known it before, I would have given you a present!" Then, with flushed face, my pouting slit prompting me, I jumped up, ran to his side and pulling my dress up to my waist, cried out: "Dear John, won't you take this? Take my virginity, I'm dying to give it to you."

"You darling girl!" he said, kissing my belly and mount. "I know that you would give it to me freely; and you know that no pleasure on earth would be as great to me as piercing your virgin womb. But think, Madge! You are so young, and some day a handsome lover will come along and you and he will marry; not until then must the dear little slit of yours be opened. No, Madge, not that. But we will celebrate the day with a revel of voluptuousness."

He filled another glass of wine and, drinking half, made me finish it. Then, ringing the bell, Meg appeared. "Take her to my room," he said, and the lively girl, putting her arm around me, danced with me to his room. "What it is, Meg? What does it mean?" She would not answer, but, leading me into a small room adjoining my uncle's, tore off every stitch of clothes she had on and then did the same to me and, naked as we were, dragged me into John's room, which was brilliantly lighted and in the center of which a narrow couch was standing, a convenient altar for sacrificing to Venus.

Leading me up to a mirror we gazed upon the reflections of our naked forms, one rosy-brown, the other rosy-white. "I guess that picture will stiffen things," she said, and, as she spoke, we heard the door open and there, facing us, stood John, naked, his lance at rest, and, beside him, Sam, his brown, muscular body bare and his magnificent pego standing bolt upright against his belly.

"Oh, I'm wild!" I cried, rushing into John's

arms. "Give relief quick!" He seized me, and laid me flat on the altar. "Give her a tongue fuck, Sam." And, in an instant, the eager mulatto was on his knees before me pressing my thighs open to their widest extent; and then, with long, pointed tongue, darting thrust on thrust into my widely stretched slit and with thick, lecherous lips, caressed the sensitive convolutions. Oh, the flashes of almost agonizing pleasure that shot through me! And when the crisis came I fairly shrieked as I spent. The three of them watched me wriggling and heaving for a moment. Then John, seizing Meg, threw her across me and said: "Now, Madge, you can see what a real fuck is like!" and for response I seized his cock and guided it into her slit. "Oh, how delicious that must be!" I shreiked. "It is," cried Meg, "give it to me harder!" and, like a horse in the stretch of a race track, John spurted. "How I feel it!" she cried, "squeeze his balls." And I did, and from a wild dance to heave and thrust, they quieted down to a gentler throbbing.

"Jolly! I can't wait," yelled Sam, holding up his burning rod. And John, taking his melting poker out of Meg's furnace, seized my hand and made me, myself, guide Sam's enormous cock into Meg's slippery slit. He was wound up and wasted no time on gentle heaves, but clutching her bottom in his hands, made his thrusts so hard and fast that the girl yelled out, "He'll knock a hole through me." But he kept on and in a second, cried: "There, you bitch, you whore, take that!" And, knowing that he was spending, I squeezed his testicles, but, overcome with my emotions, I fell back on the floor and eagerly clutched my slit in my hands.

But John snatched it away and cried out: "Come, you black rascal. Come, do what you like with this smutty virgin. Put your tongue in her and make her suck that big cock of yours." "You mean it?" cried Sam, drawing his still rampant rod out of Meg's pickling tub. But he did not wait for an answer. Like a wild animal he pounced upon me, stretching my thighs as wide as they would go and stuck his tongue deep into my coral slit; while I, frantic with lust, threw myself on his belly and seizing his still magnificent erection, sucked away every drop of sperm that was still oozing from that great rod that filled my mouth completely, until out of breath, we lay panting, our heads resting on the inside of each other's thighs, our hands gently soothing the exhausted warriors of love.

John threw himself down beside us and watched with gloating eyes, our still heaving flanks. But Meg's lustful emotions were calling loudly for assuagement. With a bound she sprang to the mantlepiece, snatched a large candle from its socket and, coming to where we three lay in a huge jumble together, she planted a foot on each side of our outstretched bodies and, in full view of our eyes, which were fixed upon her extended crevice, she plunged the candle deep into its depths, and with deft and rapid motions of her agile hand diddled herself until, exhausted, she staggered to the bed and threw herself on her back, the candle almost lost to sight.

She put her hand down to remove it, but it was in so far and so slippery that she could not get hold of it. "Oh dear, I can't get it out!" she cried. "Wouldn't it be awful if I was plugged up for good." I ran to help her, but my fingers could gain no purchase on the candle's sperm-bathed sides: so, kneeling down, I bade her open her legs to the utmost and, pressing my jaws close to her slit, I managed to catch the slippery dildo with my teeth and so draw it out.

We all laughed at this episode and Meg and I stood up and gazed down upon our two stalwart stallions still stretched upon the floor, side by side, but heads to feet. "Oh, the buggerers!" she cried. "See them feeling at each other," and so they were, each handling the other's cock. "Go on!" she cried. "All's fair in lust; I'm dying to see them suck each other!" "We will," said John, "but go and get those whips on the shelf and birch our buttocks while we taste the sweets of each other's nuts."

Wrought up, as we were by this ultra-exciting if outrageous conjuncture, we each seized a whip and, as those stalwart sodomites rolled upon their sides and with lustful lips seized each other's cocks, Meg let fall her whip upon the broad buttocks of her husband while I rained tingling blows upon John's white backsides, until it turned as rosy as my nipples.

It was disgusting—say you—perhaps it was. But to us, frenzied and drunk with all the lechery that four votaries of wantonness can, when untrammeled by prejudices, pour into each other's souls—it lost its forbidding aspects and seemed but one step further in the drama we so loved to act: *Lust a l'outrance.*

CHAPTER VIII

Time passed. Anxious to run no risks with my health, John kept me limited to weekly revels; and I was obliged at other times to recall the pleasures that had passed, or dream of what would happen when next we gave ourselves to the delightful play.

One morning John found a letter which seemed to engross him more than the others. "Well, Madge! we are going to have a visitor." "Oh, I hope not!" I said involuntarily. "It's too nice now, I hate strangers." "It can't be helped. His name is Ralph Brown, the son of my first love. His mother and I, when a little older than you are now, met and in a week we were secretly betrothed. I was summoned away on business. The last night before I left we wandered down to the shore and, seated alone there on the sand in the bright moonlight, we threw off all restraint.

"The dear girl forgot all her former modesty and did not chide me as I strained her to my breast and rained hot kisses upon her lips and shoulders. 'I am all yours,' she cried. But, wiser than to do what would be sorrow to her, I palpitated her sweet breasts and, both urged on by the same desire, I threw myself upon her panting form and, raising her skirts, my eager belly was pressed naked to hers and each, for the first time, tasted the ultimate pleasure of life; but without my penetrating her virgin bower. Again and again did we give ourselves up to these outward libations and all the pleasures that roving, eager hands could yield. I never saw her after that night. She married and they are both dead. When I was in Europe and she dying, she wrote me her last message: how she had loved me better than any other; and asking me to watch over her son. It is this son who is coming to see us. I found a good business for him in New York and, whenever he has a vacation he comes to see me. He will be here tomorrow and stay a fortnight."

He paused, and, looking at me sharply: "Why Madge, you don't seem to like the idea of his coming!" "Oh, John!" I cried, throwing my arms around his neck and kissing him, "if you are pleased, I ought to be, but—" "But what?" "Oh, we seem so happy and now we will have to be—be so very proper." "Oh ho, you minx!" he laughed and, thrusting his hand under my clothes took hold of my brush. "This is what you mean, isn't it?" "Yes, John, I shall miss it dreadfully. It's awful to be cold and proper after we have passed so many pleasant days, hot and improper." "At any rate, let us make hay while the sun shines!"

I was sitting on his knees; stooping, he grasped one of my ankles and, laughing, raised it high in the air, almost upsetting me, and brought it down on the other side. I found myself straddled across his legs. "Now, my dear little cock pleaser, strip, and let me have a little hot buff and fur to pump sperm for me." As he held a plump thigh on each side of him,

I tore off my garments and, in a minute, sat there stark naked.

Then he made me first put one leg and then the other on his shoulder. Taking off my shoes and lifting me up, he pressed my hairy mount to his face and thrust his tongue in and out of my slit. Then he sat me on a sofa and, standing between my thighs, made me unbutton his trousers and take them off, while he tore off his coat and shirt. Naked, he stood before me, his lovely pego staring me right in the face. I laid it between my bubbies, fondled its soft coat, squeezed the wrinkled storehouse of love and, beginning at the foot of the tower, kissed with open lips and caressing tongue each inch of its tall stature, until the ruby head slipped boldly into my mouth.

"You're wetting it!" he cried, and, indeed, this big mouthful did cause the saliva to secrete. "I'll be wet myself between my legs in a minute," I cried. "Yes, and your cul will be the wettest of all!" he cried, and, lifting me up, he placed me on my knees on the bed, brought his prick to the tight channel and, regardless of my squirming "Oh's" drove it in and, tickling my nipples with one hand, he rubbed my fervid slit with the other until the flood gates were opened and I was inundated with the essence of love; his behind, mine in front. Soon he rolled over on his back: "Come, glue your sticky slit to my mouth." And mounting across his face, he smothered his head between my thighs, while I, throwing myself forward, seized his sperm covered pintle in my mouth and sucked it until, breathless, I rolled over on my back and gave a long drawn cry of satisfied lechery.

CHAPTER IX

Several days later I was walking on the road, when a natural need made itself felt: I wanted to make water. Again, why say: "Make water," why not "piss," right out? Going to the side of the road, I gathered my clothes up to my waist and, squatting down, a pretty little golden puddle glistened in the sun. Rising erect and still holding my skirts up to my navel, I heard a step crackle on the dry road and, looking up, there before me stood a handsome man, seemingly in the twenties, with flashing eyes surveying my naked charms. I was spellbound, but in an instant he had his arms around my waist and a hand groping my moist mount. "Oh ho!" said he, "you're a virgin, are you? Well! you shall have it outside, if not in." And pushing me back upon a mound of grassy sward, he stood between my legs and, opening his breeches, I had one glimpse of his lovely white pego as he threw himself upon me, raining kisses on my lips, his hot staff and crisp balls delighting with quick friction my hot slit.

Of course I struggled, squirmed, kicked, and called him all sorts of names, until I felt the climax approaching to both and as I spent and could feel his sperm jetting all over my belly, I had to shut my eyes and press tight my lips to keep from showing the pleasure I was enjoying.

Springing up, he stepped back to gloat over the sight of my panting charms. With a bound I was on my feet and gathering up my dress, I sprang away and ran across the field. He followed for a moment, but soon gave it up and, calling to me: "We'll meet again, you dear," he resumed his route along the road. I hastened home and was just beginning to tell Uncle John of my adventure when a knock came, and Meg said that a gentleman wanted to see John.

CHAPTER X

Going to my room, a bath and change of dress somewhat quieted my feelings aroused by that bold stranger, and by the time that Meg came into the room to tell me that John and his guest were waiting to go to dinner, I was ready to join them, looking like a modest maiden whom a smutty word would send into convulsions.

"Ralph—this is Madge." That was the introduction, and as I looked up at him, I beheld the bold ravisher who, an hour before, had stared lustfully into my eyes while his hot sperm shot all over my belly. My heart stood still and I could hardly bow in answer to his salute, and I sank into my chair.

Fortunately, the two men had much to say to each other and I had time to gain my composure, only to have it routed again when I glanced up and found his eyes fixed upon me with the same vivid passion that had kindled my amorous soul when lying on the grass at his lustful mercy.

For three days I had no chance to be confidential with John, nor was I alone with Ralph for a minute. I avoided him. But his image was always before me. On the third day, as I was going to bed, Meg stole into my room. "Oh, Miss Madge! You ought to have seen him!" "Seen who?" I asked. "Our visitor," she said, "as I came along the hall the light was bright in his room and I couldn't help peeking through the key-hole. There he was facing the door and pulling his shirt over his head; all bare, and that lovely fresh cock of his standing stiff against his belly. I must frig myself, Miss!" And the dear girl threw herself back upon the sofa and, with her hand, rubbed the excited slit until, by her motions and glowing face, I saw that nature had come to her relief.

Of course I was on fire and, when she came to the bed and gazing down upon me, said, "Oh, wouldn't you and he make a lovely couple in bed together doing the double-backed beast in your holiday clothes?" I could stand it no longer. Pushing my naked thighs to the edge of the bed, I cried out to her to give me relief; and the kind wench soon had me thrilled with her nimble tongue and then, tucking me into bed, she left me to dream that I was part of the double-backed beast she spoke of.

I kept in my room as much as possible for I felt so awkward when I caught those bold glances of our visitor, though his manner toward me was always coldly respectful.

On the fourth day John went over to the farm-hands' quarters and I thought that Ralph had gone with him. So, going to the library, I threw myself on a sofa with a book when, from the window curtains, stepped Ralph and, standing in the middle of the floor with folded arms, he said: "Madge, I love you and want to marry you, will you have me?" My heart was in my mouth. "No, no!" I cried. "I cannot—never," and jumping to my feet, I fled to my room and threw myself sobbing, on the bed.

Did I regret the amorous dalliance with Uncle John that now arose as a barrier to the enjoyment of my new flame? No—and yet I only knew that I was miserable. I must have lain there an hour with my heart torn with conflicting emotions when I heard the door of my room pushed open and, starting up, I beheld my new lover standing, naked, with folded arms, in the middle of the room. "Madge, John has told me all. Tomorrow we will marry. I want you to come and give yourself to me now."

Oh, the revulsion of feeling! What cared I for weddings! We loved! I sprang up and with trembling hands loosed my few garments and let them drop to the floor, then started towards him with outstretched arms. He eluded me. "I want to feast my eyes for the last time upon my hot little virgin," he said. But his eager lust was not to be delayed and, seizing me in his arms, raining kisses on every part of my naked body which I returned with equal fervor, he laid me on the bed and knelt between my open legs.

"What do you want, Madge?" "I want you to make a woman of me, burst my virginity with that dear spear of yours. I shan't mind the hurt." And he was on me, his red lance aimed straight between my cunt's hot lips and forcing its way, little by little, till driven reckless by his sensations, "Brace yourself, Madge!" and, holding my bottom tightly, his iron rod burst into the useless prison and, wriggling, panting, his magnificent cock was buried to the hilt in my slit and, powerless to wait longer, his swift motion soon brought the voluptuous acme and my smarting slit was soothed by his seething sperm.

Oh, the delicious agony of the moment—pain and pleasure mixed, but the pleasure all-conquering! Oh, the languid ecstasy of lying there with his dear form pressed on breast and belly!

And, when our breath returned and he had made needed ablutions, we lay reclining side by side, how fervid the sensation of roving kiss and hand; the avidity of each to explore all the charms we had for each other. My hand had not long caressed his dear hymen breaker before its proud head was lifted again.

"Madge," he cried, lifting me up on my knees, my hairy, gaping slit before his eyes, "the second erection to enter here will not be mine. Think how your Uncle John must be suffering. Go and give him the only thing you kept from him." "No, no, Ralph. I'm yours now!" "Madge, jealousy is the cause of half the unhappiness in married life. I'll swear on this dear cunt, and you on my stiff prick, that each will love the other more than all else on earth, but that each shall take pleasure at other founts; knowing that we love each other so well that these wanton excursions will serve but as a stimulant to our mutual pleasures. I kiss the book," he said, as he pressed his lips and tongue against my slit. Then, springing up—"Now you kiss, too!" and he held the rosy headed rod to receive my ardent lips.

CHAPTER XI

"Come," he said, and leading me to John's door, Ralph opened it and, pushing me in, closed it softly. I advance quietly to the head of the bed where I had so often tasted nameless sweets, and gazed down upon John's nude form, stretched there on his back, his mind filled no doubt with vivid pictures of the voluptuous drama being enacted at the other end of the hall and holding the inflamed arrow of love erect in his hand.

"Ralph sent me, John. He has ravished my virginity and swears that he won't fuck me again until your sperm mixes with his in my belly." "You darling girl! Do you mean it?" and wildly seizing me in his arms he threw me flat on my back and, kneeling between my thighs I grasped his dear old cock in my hand and, myself, guided it to my newly opened quiver.

Oh, that rapture giving tongue, fucking my mouth; that stiff strong prick fucking my cunt; that thrilling flood of boiling sperm shooting at last into its proper channel and now, for the first time, sending bliss to my innermost vitals. How we squirmed and twisted in our lustful embrace and how happy and content we lay, regaining our breath, till a voice at our side roused us.

"Did you enjoy it?" and looking up, there

stood Ralph in all his naked, manly beauty, his pego up in arms. Quickly raising himself, John held out his hand, which Ralph grasped, while I, seizing them both, pressed them, joined together, to my happy slit. Then I sprang up and with an arm around each manly form I kissed first one, then the other, and exclaimed: "Oh! how happy I am with two such lovers!" "Let us look at ourselves," said John, and, with encircling arms, we ran up to the mirror and gazed with lustful eyes on the splendid picture of our naked charms.

"On your knees and worship Priapus," said Ralph. As I dropped on my knees, he turned my head to John's pego, which I quickly seized in my mouth, and which quickly stiffened; and then, with eager lips, I turned to kiss the rampant rooster that had just crowed for the first time—in my virgin belly.

Raising me, they made me stand straddled on two chairs and, each in turn, standing under my crotch, thrust his tongue into my quiver. "This is too much, how I wish I had two cunts, so as to have both fuck me at once!" "You know you have!" said John, "didn't I take your 'maiden-behind' and Ralph your maidenhead?" "Let's put both in at once!" cried Ralph and, making me stoop, his rigid rod was soon engulfed in my excited slit, when John, lifting up my legs, crossed them tightly around Ralph's waist and I was suspended there—hung upon a peg, as it were—while John, pointing his spear against my well-stretched bottom, pierced me to the hilt.

Oh! The wild shouts of agonizing rapture that deluged me as those two lusty darts of love were driven with simultaneous thrusts into my quivering body, and as the double dose of sperm was shot, like molten lead, into me, I shrieked aloud till Ralph's nimble tongue, with prick-like stiffness, was urged into my cunt-like mouth and I sucked it, as my contracting slit and cul sucked from their pricks the last lovely drops of sperm.

I almost fainted as they laid me on the bed; but a good stiff horn of whiskey poured down my throat revived me, and bathed with spirits, I soon lay happy across Ralph's lap on the sofa while John, lighting a cigar, sat naked in an easy chair opposite us and told us smutty incidents of his life.

CHAPTER XII

Meg and Sam kept in the background since Ralph appeared. But I had not forgotten them. One day, after we had rested after the effects of our razzle-dazzle, John was away and Ralph, as we left the table, lit his cigar and, groping me, told me to go to my room and strip and, as soon as he finished smoking, he would come and we would have a nice, quiet little diddle all by ourselves.

I pressed the bulging balls in his breeches and going to my room, threw myself naked on the bed to wait for him. Just then Meg passed the door and I called her in. I had been too busy with my own slit and Ralph's and John's dear cocks to think of her or Sam, but, as she stood by the bed, I sprang up and embraced her. "Oh Meg, forgive me! We've been so busy with ourselves. Come strip, get into bed with me and when Ralph comes, I'll make him give you a taste of his old gentleman." "No, no, Miss Madge, he is all yours!" But I jumped up and commenced tearing off her clothes.

Just as I, standing upon the bed, was pulling her chemise over her head, Ralph entered.

"See how two girls can enjoy each other!" I cried, and I threw the wench on the bed and, with mouths glued to each other's slits, we gave him a lively duet of tongue thrusting. While watching us he stripped and, as we lay languidly, side by side, he approached and examined my dusky bed-fellow. "What a nice, plump little brown Venus it is!" he said, as his hands roved over her. "Leave me alone," she said, "you belong to Miss Madge."

But I took Ralph's prick in my hand and held it up, rigid and fierce: "Do you mean to tell me you don't want a taste of this?" I asked. "Oh, I do, Miss. I do. My slit's hot now!"

"Get on your knees," I cried, "so that I can see the whole race up and down your hairy place!" and the lusty wench did as I told her, and, giving Ralph's rooster a parting kiss, I pointed it for her center of attraction and gave myself up to the delightful spectacle of their lusty working bung and spigot, and, when Meg's well-filled belly rolled, squirming, upon the bed, I clasped Ralph's loins in my hands and took the fallen monarch in my mouth, sucking into me the last drop.

"One of you must tongue tickle me, quick!" I cried. "Hold on!" said Ralph, snatching away his hand which I had clasped against my slit. "Where's that robust husband of yours, Meg? Go and fetch him and tell him there's a lady here who wants the use of his cock for a few minutes." "Shall I Miss?" cried the delighted wench, springing to her feet. "Hurry up!" said Ralph, and he gave her plump backside a resounding smack with his hand as the girl sprang naked out of the door.

"Oh, Ralph! do you really want me to let that black man fuck me?" I asked. "I know you have let him kiss my slit and suck it, and I've kissed him too, and twice he went off in my mouth; but, if he fucks me straight, I might have a brown baby." Ralph laughed aloud.

"Black babies or not," he cried, "I'm going to see that big muscular fellow fuck you right up to the handle," and he threw himself on the bed and pulled me down, with my rump on the edge, tickling my nipples and clitoris as I lay across him.

A moment thus and, in the doorway, appeared the sprightly wench, and, beside her, the magnificently muscular and manly form of Sam. He was a little bashful at this sudden introduction into such company, but the royal prick that the wench held in her hand showed how excited his passions were.

"See, Miss!" cried she, "isn't it a whopper?" "Walk up to the captain's office and settle!" cried Ralph. And, as the big darky advanced and stood between my thighs I lost all my fears and took the splendid specimen of virility in my hand. "What a monster he is!" I cried. "He's grown bigger than ever!" "Jolly, Miss," said Meg, "he's had lots of exercise since you and Massa John and Massa Ralph have been fucking and sucking each other all over the house. We had to peep in sometimes and see you three fooling with each other, and this black rascal when you all came to the going off point, would make me get down on my knees and suck him while he watched you three wriggling." "You wicked peeper!" I cried. "I'll pay you for that! Go and get that whip Meg, and thrash his backsides." And I guided his immense prick between the lips of my slit and threw myself back, panting, to taste this luscious morsel.

"Quat her just as you would Meg!" cried Ralph, and seizing my bum the lusty black thrust that soul-satisfying shaft of his plump rod up to the hilt. "Oh, it's splendid! It's a splitter, don't spare me, it's so lovely! Don't hold back! That's it! Oh, it's so good. Faster! I'll keep time with you! Whip his buttocks harder! Oh, he's swelling! I'm coming! Squeeze his balls, Ralph! Oh! Oh!" and heaving wildly, clutching the bedclothes with my hands, working my bottom as if dancing on a hot stove, my cunt, chock-full of that rigid, robust mountain of hard flesh, I yelled with delight, frantically threw up my legs and, closing them around him, kicked his bottom with my heels, until he cried: "Now it flies! Take that in your womb, and that, and that"—and the frantic Hercules forgetting all but that we were two animals in lecherous agony, yelled at me: "You want fucking, do you; you want your belly full? Ain't you getting it? Take that! Suck every drop out with your puckering cunt, my pretty diddler!"

And I, wriggling, shrieking, and quivering with lust, called to him: "Oh, it's heaven! My insides are flooded: I feel the sperm drops burn me as they hit my belly! I'm riddled with hot shots! Give me every charge in your gun! My buttocks are going and I can't stop. Whip him some more."

For he had quieted his rapid motions. "Yes!" he yelled. "Flog me harder and I'll give her another dose without coming out!" "You mean it?" I cried. For all response he seized me in his arms lifted me up still spiked on his prick, and ran around the room with me; squeezing my backsides, putting his finger in my cul, thrusting his tongue in my mouth, and nibbling at my nipples while I sucked his tongue and clasped him tightly with arms and loins while Meg whipped both our bottoms until, at length, I again felt the thrill of his stiffening pego and, laying me again on the bed, he worked his heavenly probe in and out of my slit until I felt the great drops fly once again into me and with a shriek I fainted.

CHAPTER XIII

When I came to myself in bed in my darkened room, Ralph, all dressed, sat by my side while I clasped his neck in my arms.

"Madge, you are young yet, and new to voluptuous raptures. You've been going at it too hard. We have been selfish in spurring you on so fast. Gradually you will become hardened to amorous play and be able to bear all that we can give and take together. But now you need a rest and you must obey and leave that sensitive slit of yours alone for four days, or until Sunday. And, Madge, you mustn't excite John and I by going around with your lovely bubbies bare, or letting us see your lovely legs. It's pretty hard to swear off even for a few days. But, for the sake of your health, we must all sacrifice ourselves."

I kissed the dear fellow and promised to obey him; so we passed three highly respectable days, walking, riding and avoiding all temptations until on Saturday night, I went to bed in perfect health and yearning eagerly to again feel that blissful balm in my belly.

When I awoke in the morning my thing quickly reminded me that its itching was again to be solaced and, as I raised myself on my elbow, I gazed with gloating eyes down on that dear handsome lover of mine stretched out in bed on his back, still sleeping.

Gently I raised his nightshirt and feasted my eyes upon his innocent looking love shaft lying softly on the cushion-like testicles. Involuntarily my hand slid down over his belly and gently caressed the wrinkled weapon of lustful warfare.

Taking it in my fingers, with soft, quiet touches along its length, I saw, with flushing eyes and puckering slit, its softness swelled to stiffness, and soon my hand was filled with the rich rotundity of a glorious erection and my gloated eyes feasted on the round, red head, gorged with blood, and the gaping slit on its top, looking ready to spurt forth a shower of sperm.

Getting quickly onto my knees I drew my nightdress over my head and, without touching, straddled across him. Then, taking his prick in my hand, I held it bolt upright and, settling my body down upon it, it was soon piercing my vagina. In an instant a lustful, upward jerk of his buttocks made it disappear in my hole, and, glancing down, I saw that Ralph was awake and, with ardent gaze, watching my performances.

"Oh, you young lecherer! You couldn't wait until I woke up, but must ravish me in my sleep!" he laughed. "You've kept me on short commons long enough," I answered, "and now I'm going to feast my belly full." "Well, go ahead!" he cried, "but you must do all the work yourself. Wait a second until I stuff this pillow under me; it will help give you a longer stroke."

As I commenced to work my thighs with rapid, ravishing heaves upon his stately prick, he cried out to me: "Go to it, my pretty wench, my lovely, lusty lecherer, my sweet suction pump, my coral-cunted cock-pleaser, my dear whore, my ever ready sperm churner; wag your tail my lascivious little buttock worker! Push your slit tight on my belly, keep on—faster—faster!" Until, with a sudden spring forward he caught my bum in his hands and, with the burst of ultimate passion, threw me over on my back and, with straining muscles and bursting veins, gave me those sweet, final thrusts with such rapturous rapidity that my long stored juices oozed out around his pubes and wet his balls.

"I heard that hot-bellied cry way out in my room," said a voice, and looking up, Uncle John stood by the bedside watching us with lustful eyes.

"She's got a fine action in her bum, John," cried Ralph, "let her pump up your sperm, herself." And John, lying down with his buttocks on a settee, held his darling staff straight up in the air. Ralph lifted me astride of him while I put his cock where it would do the most good. I had just commenced working my thighs when Ralph, seeing a riding whip on the table, let it fall in tingling blows on my high lifted bottom until the excitement of the fight made his own cock get a hard-on and, tackling me behind, he stuck it in my cul while John was struggling to his feet. They both stood upright with me between them, lifted on their stiff staffs and having my whole body thrilled by their eager thrusts and copious shots of sperm.

As we rested and I lay there with two birds in my hand and sure of having them both in my bush, also, "How shall we do it next?" I cried. "Shall I tell you," said John, "how I first took a diddle?" "That will be splendid!" I cried. And, settling ourselves in each other's way together, their hands gently caressing my slit and I holding in each hand the two pretty nightingales that had sung so often and so sweetly for me, he began.

CHAPTER XIV

"At sixteen I was a virgin. The sexual sensation had never been experienced and, if I had any amorous longings I did not know what they meant and my pintle was simply a piss-passer for me.

"One day I was climbing a smooth cherry tree, about as large around as Madge's waist, and, as I climbed up, with my arms and legs clasped tightly against it and rubbing up and down, my cock stiffened and a new sensation began to steal over me.

"Wondering what it was, I held the tree still tighter, instinctively, and worked my buttocks. Soon a delicious feeling spread all over me and centered itself in my prick, and as I kept on with faster heavings, I felt it stiffen in my breeches and soon it seemed to burst and shoot out something, I knew not what, while I felt that my belly was wet and a delightful languor spread over my whole body. I was astounded and clutched the tree until, too weak to hold on any longer, I slid to the ground. Lying there, I opened my breeches and found myself all covered with some sticky substance I had never seen before.

"I was half frightened, and went home and, stripping, washed myself and got on the bed, resolved to try if I could not recall those delicious feelings.

"As I took my cock in my hand and played with it I soon found that it grew bigger and bigger. It was soon stiff and swollen while the skin, which hid the head, soon yielded in a vigorous downward motion leaving the cap of love rosy and exposed.

"I did not know but what I had injured myself, but, spurred on by the exquisite pleasure I soon found my frigging hand made, I worked the skin up and down, faster and faster, and soon the same sensation which I had experienced on the tree stole over me. I felt something inside giving away and, in a delirium of delight, saw, for the first time, the milky seed fly high in the air and, keeping up the friction, squeezed out the last drop and lay back, panting.

"My eyes were half open. As I thought of this phenomena I wondered what it all meant until, one day, I saw our buxom servant girl leave the kitchen and, looking all around as if to see if she was watched, go into the barn.

"I followed, and, glueing my eyes to the wide crack in the boards, saw another crack that made my prick so stiff as to almost split my breeches open. The girl was in heat, had thrown herself, half reclining on her back, upon the hay full front to where I was peeping and had pulled her clothes up to her waist.

"I fastened my eyes on her broad hips and fleshy thighs, her fat, round belly heaving up and down, and the great mass of black, curly hair which was plainly in view between her outstretched thighs. Her face had an eager expression as she fixed her eyes upon her excited center and, I quickly saw her hide it from view with her hand and, with extended fingers, rub herself up and down, seeming to penetrate into some opening there.

"Instinctively I tore open my trousers and, taking my cock in my hand, kept time with her self-deflowering motions until I heard her give forth a half-suppressed cry of satisfaction, heaving her hips more wildly and working her hand faster, spending, just as my own agile hand pumped out the white sperm that flew high up on the barn toward her.

"After that I kept my eye on her and, whenever I saw her go off by herself to the barn or bedroom, I quickly followed and, gloating over the sight of her naked charms and lewd actions, joined her, unseen, in a revel of masturbation.

"In fact, I jerked myself off so often that I grew thin and weak and my father, not knowing the cause, wrote to a young curate whom he knew and sent me off to his distant parsonage for a change of air and to continue my studies under his care.

"The minister was an athletic young fellow of thirty and lived alone with his wife, a bright, pleasant faced, plump figured girl of twenty-two, overflowing with animal spirits and jolly, but proper and discreet, as became her position.

"For a week or so I left my cock alone. I was bashful, as I said, and the novelty of my surroundings kept me thinking of other things.

"But, passing her door one day, when she said she was going to take a bath, I couldn't resist peeping through the key-hole. There she stood, naked and lovely, sponging herself briskly with a towel; lifting one plump leg upon a chair, her naked, wide stretched thighs open to my eager eyes.

"I yielded to the fires that were burning within me and rushing to my room, ran to the open window and shot a full libation of sperm into the glistening sunlight.

"And I kept it up for a week until one day after dinner, when we were all in the library —the young dominie sat on the sofa and his wife on his lap—while I, opposite them at the window, pretended to be reading but was, in fact, furtively gazing with a carnal eye at the trim ankles and plump calves of his wife that her reclining attitude brought into view.

" 'John,' said the dominie, 'I've got something to say to you. I know how I suffered at your age and I see you wrecking your health and want to save you.' 'What do you mean?' I asked. 'You know what I mean,' he answered kindly. And my flushed face answered him. 'I've suspected that you were playing with yourself for some time, but yesterday, Mollie, here, saw you jerking yourself off in your room. Now, I've a proposition to make to you. If you will promise me on your honor, never to masturbate again while you are here—once a week, Mollie will let you do anything you like with her. In plain English, today is Friday; every Friday you may fuck Mollie to your heart's content, but for the rest of the week, you must leave lewdness entirely alone. Do you promise?' 'Do you mean it?' I cried, jumping to my feet, my cock stiff in my breeches. 'Doesn't this look like I meant it?' he said, and seizing his blushing wife, he drew her across his lap as he lay extended on the sofa and, pulling up her clothes as high as they would go, exposed to my eyes her lovely body, naked from the waist down. 'On your knees between her legs and swear to keep your promise,' said the dominie. And kneeling there she seized my hand, pushed it down upon her lovely mount. 'Kiss the book,' she said. I was only a second there, for I was ready to spend, when rising to my feet, the lovely girl quickly unbuttoned my breeches and taking my over-excited prick in her hand guided it quickly into her slit. 'Fuck me!' she said. 'Fuck me! I want it as much as you do!' And, eagerly grasping her bottom, I felt my pego pierce her tight crevice and enter her completely until belly touched belly and her hair curled in mine. I could not speak. I simply uttered an inarticulate cry of joy and commenced working in and out, as I had been taught by my frigging hand.

" 'There! You naughty boy, isn't that nicer than playing with yourself?' And, throwing her arms around her husband's neck—'Are you jealous, hubby?' 'Jealous?' he cried. 'It's delicious! I enjoy the sight as much as you do the act. Give it to her, John!' 'It's coming,' I cried. 'I am too,' she answered. 'Tickle the top of my slit, hubby.' And the dear girl took my virgin offering deep into the recesses of her gaping womb.

"Then, reaching up she threw her arms around my neck and drew me down upon her, as we rained passionate kisses on each other. 'Come!' cried the husband. 'Let's have a Garden of Eden. Quick, run to your rooms, strip and come back. Hurry up, see in what a state I am!' and he held up his big prick ready to burst.

"In two minutes there were two Adams and one Eve; and at once, Eve, making me lie on the sofa, threw herself across me and, taking the big pego of the original Adam, the handsome couple were soon pumping sperm at each other. Resting from their labors the lovely girl caught sight of my prick, which was sticking up stiff again. 'See this wicked young cock, it is ready to crow again!'

"As I rolled off of her, her husband sprang forward. 'By Priapus, Mollie,' he called, 'now you have been taken in adultery you shall do what you have refused to do—suck my cock.' 'Yes, indeed, I will!' she cried. 'Sit on the floor, then, between John's legs,' he said, and her backsides were soon close to my belly while he, kneeling before her, stuck his great, inflamed cock invitingly into her face. Quickly her open lips closed over the ruby head and slid down the huge column, while one hand clutched his bum, and the other his testicles. 'Work your lips just as you do your slit,' he cried. What a luscious sight it was, but so short. 'There it comes,' and the swollen glands told that he was spending. Taking her hand away a minute, the sperm flew over her and over me, and then, seizing it again in her mouth, she did not let go until, with a deep sigh of satisfied emotion, he, himself, withdrew, melted by the fervor of her lips, tongue, and inhaling breath."

CHAPTER XV

As John finished the narrative of his initiation into the mysteries of Venus the two nightingales in my hands held their necks up straight in the air and their little, gaping mouths looked ready to sing. My lustful imagination, excited by all that I had experienced, wandered into unknown realms of lechery.

"How do men like priests, sailors and soldiers, shut off from women, satisfy their voluptuous longings?" I asked. "You forget, Madge," said Ralph, "that John and I tasted each other's sweets the other day." "Yes," said John, "they do that and fuck each other's culs. I remember that once, in a house party in New Orleans, a party of us had been treated exhaustively by a bevy of licentious creole girls and were lying around in all sorts of lewd attitudes, when the buxom mistress of the house came in and, standing naked there, clapped her hands for silence. 'You all know, that my business in life is to please my patrons with novelties and I have arranged this evening an act which I will call 'A Half Hour in Sodom.'

"Going to the door she opened it and into the center of the room marched ten men, in single file, like soldiers. They were young and middle aged, ten splendidly formed, naked creoles or mulattoes, carrying their stiff pegos at 'present arms' before them.

"The mistress knelt on the floor, her splendid buttocks thrust out, and the first darky put his prick into the hole of her fleshy arse; then the second man's cock entered her cul, and so on to the last man, making a chain of buggering lustfulness that was a delicious morsel to our highly seasoned palates.

"As they worked their cocks into each other they kept shouting smutty talk; and when the spending came, the whole line trembled like a ship in a storm and those ten athletic bodies wriggling, writhing, panting, yelling, in a complete surrender to their most licentious instincts, was a sight beyond which the lewdest imagination can go."

John's story, and the voluptuous touches we had experienced from each other's hands and lips, brought the moment when we must get rid of the cream that their licentiousness had distilled.

Holding Ralph's darling diddler in one hand, I pressed the cheeks of his bottom with the other. "Ralph, I believe that that old sodomite there wants to put his prick in here." "Why not?" said Ralph. "Glorious," said John, and, seizing me he threw me on the edge of the bed and stuck Ralph's immense erection deep into my slit. "Wet the head in your mouth," he said, and I made his eager prick slippery with saliva. In an instant, it was pointed at Ralph's tight and virgin cul.

All the struggle to get it in heightened my own pleasure, for it made Ralph's prick swell bigger and throb deliciously in my happy sheath.

Finally John, unable to curb his lust longer, tore Ralph's bottom with a mighty thrust, and three bellies and buttocks were moving wildly together in lustful unison until, in blissful agony, I lay sweltering in licentious lassitude, with my two dear stallions in a heap on top of me.

CHAPTER XVI

From the time when Ralph first rid me of my burdensome and hateful maidenhead—carried it away on the point of his lance—I had never so much as thought of marriage. Our entwined arms and legs and his dear shaft nailing me down to the couch of pleasure were all the bonds I cared for. But, before long, he had to return to New York. I hardly dared think of it; we had been so full of the present, at least I had been so full of their doings. One day I had been walking alone and, returning, found Ralph and John talking seriously. They seated me on the sofa between them but didn't put their hands in my bosom or under my skirts. I was really frightened; I thought that something had happened and looked anxiously from one to the other.

"Madge, Ralph and I have been talking about the future. I have business that will take me to the Pacific in a few days and Ralph must return to New York and you must go with him." "Oh!" I cried, "I knew we couldn't go on always as we are—but . . . " I got no further, buried my face in my hands, and burst into tears.

To leave John was bitter, but since the night that he first possessed me, I had held Ralph in my heart, as so-called virtuous women do their husbands.

"Yes, Madge, Ralph and I have decided that you and he be legally married and go and live in New York." "Oh John, it's like taking half of my life away to leave you." "Of course, it seems so," said Ralph, "but John can visit us often, and we him." And it was all settled.

One evening, not long after, I had gone to my room for something when Meg appeared, entirely naked, and said: "Miss Madge, they want you in the parlor, in the same clothes I have on." "Oh Meg," I said, "I suppose they want us to take some of the starch out of them." "It's more than that, Miss." And, curious, I stripped and followed her.

The room was brilliantly lighted. At the head of a couch in the center, stood a priest, book in hand, while behind him, were Ralph, John and Sam, all three as bare as Meg and I.

I stood still with wonder; when John came forward and, leading me to the couch, threw me on my back. Then Ralph came forward and stood between my legs, his arrow aimed at my bull's-eye.

The priest stood at the side and, opening his book, commenced the short marriage service and, as he pronounced the declaration that we were man and wife, he took my hand and, making me grasp my newly-made husband's prick, guided it into my slit. The dear fellow gave me a hard trot and, foundering at the end, invited John to follow him, which he did.

Then Ralph asked the priest to give me his blessing and the holy man, advancing to the altar, presented to our view a Priapus of immense size and got between my legs. "Will you accept my blessing," he asked, "and let me anoint you with the holy oils?" "Oh, Father, pour oil on my troubled waters." And that stalwart prick of his went plunging into me and kept pounding away until a profuse scattering of his sanctified sperm sent me off, wriggling, like a fish on a hook.

Then Ralph, turning to Sam, said: "There is no black or white in heaven and her slit is at present heaven." The well wound up and richly adorned darky gave me a diddle that, for size of cock, vigor of action, and copious spending, was as perfect as the lovely grotto of Venus itself could have wished for.

CHAPTER XVII

But I must close my adventure in this land of the bayous. A few days before Ralph and I were to turn our faces to the north, John and I were out walking along a secluded road, when we came upon a small hovel such as the free Negroes occupy. "Come here Madge, let me fuck you!" in a man's voice, startled us, but John motioned me to keep quiet. We stole up to a clump of bushes surrounding a little yard and there, stretched on a grassy bank, was a big, burly Negro, stark naked and holding up a cock that would have served the womb of nature itself and beget all her fruits. Capering before him were two immense dogs—as big as young colts and one mass of muscle. As usual now, my thoughts were sexual and I saw that one was a bitch and the other a dog.

"Come, my little Madge!" and the bitch, barking, came up to him. Getting behind her, her tail standing up and showing her slit, the buggering black pointed his prick at it and plunged it in almost to the hilt. The bitch barked and wriggled and the Negro, his face aglow with lust, kept crying between his teeth: "Ah, my nice whore, you're better than a girl; your slit fits my cock like a glove, now I must squirt!" and, working his immense bum, I saw by the contractions of his muscles, that he was spending into the slit.

My cunt was burning at this novel, if outrageous scene and I thrust out my hand and grasped John's staff, stiff in his breeches. "Wait," he whispered, "let's see it through." The black threw himself on his back, his great prick prone, but a giant, even in its fall. "Come Rover!" he cried. And the dog, who had been jumping around the lusty pair and whose cock stuck out stiff under his belly, its crimson head plainly visible, came prancing up to him, barking frantically.

Quickly getting his wooly head under the dog's belly we saw him grasp the canine's penis and suck it while the dog wiggled his hind quarters and gave a wail of pleasure as the black sucked the juice out of him.

Frantic with lust, John tore open his breeches, seized me in his arms and, rushing with me to the grassy knoll on which the buggering black lay, threw up my clothes and in an instant was fucking me like mad.

The frightened black sprang to his feet, but our stroking match made him forget his fears and, standing over us, he watched our lustful enjoyment with shining eyes.

Weltering in our completed conjunction, John seized me, tore off all my clothes and holding my parting thighs out invitingly to the black, cried: "There, you black buggerer! Isn't that nicer to fuck than a slut?" "What do you mean, Massa? You let me fuck that lovely white cunt?" "Come, show her your prick and ask her!" And the Negro stood between my legs and I held in my hand one of nature's masterpieces—the thought of which makes me feel like masturbating.

"Oh! It's too big! I'm afraid of it!" "Bosh!"

cried John, "a woman's slit is elastic enough to swallow an elephant." And driven by desire, I grasped that enormous prick in my hand and in an instant it was stretching wide my vagina and knocking deliciously at my womb. Oh! the wild animal cries of a lecherous stallion! The frantic clutching of my heaving bum! The wild thrusting of that immense probe in and out of my distended cunt! Then, the fierce energy of the final swelling and the lecherous agony of the hot sperm shooting all through my belly and sucking from me all the slimy overflow of my over-excited being!

I lay back limp. "Some water, quick!" and the black sprang away and in a second was back and dashing it into my face. I soon revived.

"I didn't mean to hurt you, Miss." "Hurt me? It was too heavenly! Come here and let me handle that gift of the Gods." And leaning against John I gloated over that splendid engine of love as he knelt by my side.

"Why do you keep that for brutes instead of women?" "Because good women are afraid of me and the bad women I've had live with me robbed me, poor as I am. I got disgusted and have lived here alone for a year. Slut ain't bad," he said, and, turning to John, whose prick was stiff: "Try Madge!" and called the big bitch to him and fondled her.

"Go on, John!" I cried; and he, jumping to his knees, pulled the bitch up to his belly sternwise and I, myself, pointed his dart into her. "It's like a young girl's cunt!" he said, "Splendid!" And the rapid motions soon told that the tightness of the orifice was bringing on the climax and I put my hand out and squeezed his balls as he shot his sperm into the bitch's haunches.

While this was going on the dog was going around smelling the bitch and John's prick. Now the black seized him and lifted him up by the hind legs and in this position he was almost as tall as the darky. His cock was stiff and the crisp little balls somehow made my slit contract. "Let him fuck you, Miss!" cried the lewd black. "By Jove, she shall!" said John, and seizing me, he pushed me down on my knees and pulled me way back against him until my hairy slit stuck out just at the right height for my canine lover. He walked the dog up to me on his hind legs, and stood him upright between my legs like a man while the Negro pressed him close to my slit and directed his prick into it.

Not its size—a small cock often gives more pleasure than a big one—but the novel lechery of the scene excited my lust and I was working my bottom when John called, "Let the dog cover her as he would a bitch!" The darky threw the dog down, its breast against my belly and his legs clutching my sides, while, thoroughly in heat, he worked his loins rapidly. My feelings touched a new kink in licentiousness, when, with a low bark, he shot his sperm into me. I threw myself back on the grass quivering. "Oh, that's only an appetizer; give me something more substantial; my slit is burning." "How's that?" cried the black, kneeling over my chest, his awful erection staring me full in the face. "Oh, it's lovely!" and I squeezed his coconut-like balls, grasped the firm staff in my hand, gently frigged it and took its enormous head in my mouth. It was a mouthful, and I had given it but a few sucks when the excited engine exploded and the hot drops flew into my mouth.

I threw myself back: "Quick, into my slit!" I cried. Wild with spending agony, this lovely son of Priapus threw himself upon me, his sperm jutting out all over me until, plunged safely in my slit, he poured into the innermost crevices a volume of the burning fluid that set my buttocks in motion, wildly eager to catch every drop, and compelled from me a flow of all my being, poured down in welcome to this prince of fuckers.

CHAPTER XVIII

And now the last night together came, and I suppose that you must anticipate a wholesale razzle-dazzle; but John and I felt the parting too keenly.

Ralph and I were in our room and I had just dropped my chemise and was sitting, naked, pulling off my stockings. "Madge, go to John's bed and spend the night in his arms." I kissed him fondly and went. Not forgetful of him, I ran to Meg's room, told her where I was going to pass the night and bade her go down to Ralph and see if he did not want to have a stroking match with her before he went to sleep.

Then I hastened to John, and entering the familiar room found it dark and he in bed. "What's that?" "Me, dear John; I've come to spend the night." And, wrapped in his arms like a child in its father's, or a bride in her husband's, half tearful and half rapturous with our soft pleasures, I fell asleep on his breast.

Morning found us there, inhaling our souls into each other's lips, glued together, bellies throbbing and his dear shaft carrying soft rapture to my inner soul, until, in the ecstasy of our last embrace a knock came, and Sam entered with John's shaving water.

"Sam, you must say good-by," and soon his stalwart pego was buried within me and twice shot its elixer into my womb; the second time while I drew from John's dear staff the last libation of love.

Three hours later Ralph and I were on a train for the north.

The express was crowded, but finally the conductor came and told us a director of the road was occupying a state-room, and had consented to share it with us.

We found it a pretty apartment, shut from the rest of the car, with mirrors and carpets, easy chairs and an inviting looking sofa.

The occupant was a handsome man of fifty, and very courteous, "I fear we shall disturb you," said Ralph. "No, I was getting lonesome and you are more than welcome to join me as far as Philadelphia where this car will be switched off."

I threw myself on the sofa and watched the moving panorama as we passed the morning in pleasant talk. Once I caught my host's eyes, fixed with a gleam on my plump leg, which in changing position I had exposed.

When we stopped for dinner the two gentlemen alighted, brought me a lunch, and then promenaded the platform.

The train started again, when Ralph said: "Madge, our host and I have been confidental; you ought to have heard the compliments he made of you! Go sit on his lap, and tell him he can have what he wants." "Stop your nonsense," I said. But the laughing rascal took me in his arms and placed me in our host's lap.

"Won't you be kind to an amorous old codger and stay?" "Yes, I will and I will make Ralph jealous!" I cried. And throwing my arms around my new lover's neck, I gave him a kiss.

I could feel his staff stiffen against my bottom and his hand instinctively pressed my breast. "There, you naughty fellow! You shall have them at discretion," and with both hands I lifted my plump titties out of my clothes and, with a cry of pleasure, he covered them with kisses.

"Pull up her petticoats and I will show you the way into her," said Ralph, and, jumping up, he let loose his prick, fully recovered from Meg's drubbing.

"Bravo!" cried our host, and quickly snatching up all that hid my lovely legs, thighs and belly, as he called them, my bottom was clasped in Ralph's hands and his staff was knocking at my slit.

"May I put it in?" said our host. "Of course you may," and he guided it in. "You can squeeze his balls too, if you want to," and he did. Seeing that we were spending he pushed his head down and with clinging lips and tongue, kissed and tickled my hot clitoris and Ralph's lunging shaft until, as it was withdrawn, the sperm still oozing from its gaping nozzle, he, unable to control himself, seized it in his mouth and sucked it. Fired by his emotions, he sprang to his feet, tore open his trousers and showed me a new morsel to be devoured by my hungry slit.

Ralph stretched me on my back on the floor, naked from the waist, and my gray-haired but virile companion was in a moment a prisoner in my belly—a lively one, too—dancing like mad up and down, while I imprisoned his whole body with arms and legs until we both experienced the most delicious novelty of a first diddle between a congenial man and woman.

When we resumed the role of respectable members of society there wasn't a drop of love juice in either of them.

CHAPTER XIX

Reaching New York, we quickly settled down in the plain but cosy little flat that Ralph had, by writing, made ready for us.

A month passed in all the quiet pleasures of the usual newly married couple.

Then our first trouble came. We had spent all our money in fitting up our apartment and seeing the sights. John was too far away to help and we hated to borrow, and could only wait for Ralph's salary to come due.

Our landlord was a man—a muscular little hunchback of forty—who lived in bachelor quarters in the first flat.

He had been pleasant enough; but now, after calling two or three times for the money and receiving only excuses he began to grow angry and made us uncomfortable.

One morning, after Ralph had gone, a note was stuck under the door. He wrote that if he did not receive the rent that day we would have to move. I threw myself on the bed and burst into tears. Our cosy nest torn to pieces perhaps. Something must be done. Arranging myself, I decided to brave the little misformed lion in his den, all by myself.

Trembling, I knocked at his door. He called: "Come in." I found him writing at a table.

Standing opposite, I made my plea and begged him to wait a little longer and not break up our new home. The man was silent, but his bright, piercing eyes seemed to burn as they wandered over my person, which a chemise and a thin wrapper draped, but did not hide, the contour of.

He arose and, going to a window, gazed out with his back to me. Then he broke the silence. "Madame, I am a man of business; debts are debts and must be paid. But I am also, a pleasure-seeker. If you are offended you can return to your room. Ever since you came into the house I have desired to possess you; watched you as you mounted the stairs, catching glimpses of your trim legs, and twice I have watched you and your husband, like youthful Venus and Mars, give your bodies up to each other's enjoyment, and causing my seed to be spilled on the ground. I am an ugly dwarf I know, more to be loathed than loved, but if you can forget your handsome lover and yield to my ardor, every outpouring will count to you a month's rent paid."

"Never! I never sold myself, but— " and I hesitated and threw myself into a great sleepy hollow chair. He stood facing me. "But what?" "If you love a man for love's sake, yea, for lust's sake—" I did not finish, but, stretching out my legs as I reclined, I unbuttoned my wrapper and lay there, a tempting bit of fluff and fur from waist to heels.

"You splendid creature!" he cried, and, throwing himself on his knees between my thighs, kissed belly, legs and mount, but only for a second; then he jumped to his feet, stripped open his breeches and showed me the first circumcised cock I had ever seen. The great head was more freely exposed than a

Christian's; it was of a length and thickness that recalled the immense erections of those black lovers of mine in the South.

"It's as big as you are!" I cried. Quickly aiming it at my excited target, he drove it in and, with athletic thrusts soon made me show, with wildly working belly, that I wasn't being fucked for cold cash, but was as eager as he was to exchange with him the white coinage of concupiscence.

"You're a very priestess of enjoyment," he cried, and lifting me up in his strong arms he sat where I had been, and I lay straddled across him, his prick still in, his lips sucking my nipples. "Oh," I cried, "that was delicious." "What would your husband say if he saw us here?"

"Do you think I would have let you, if he would object?"

And I told him how we were devoid of prejudices and each gladly yielded the mate to the lascivious pleasings of others.

"After my own heart! Why this clap-trap of fidelity, making necessity for brothels and adulteries leading oft to murder? Why shouldn't a man and woman who fancy each other shake cocks and cunts together as well as hands? But come, my Venus, let me see you in true Venus costume." And, devoured by his lustful gaze, I dropped the last veil and he likewise.

But he had heavy shoulders, muscular arms and legs, great, bulging buttocks—and, oh! —that cock, which was already recovering. Pressing me down upon the bed, he fixed his head between my thighs and, with admiring words and enlivening touches, examined the sheath of his pleasures. "I, too, like to know about the tools I use," I said. He quickly knelt across my chest, and I fondled and caressed his enormous prick until he seized me and, with my weight resting on my bubby cushions, my bottom raised, he, standing behind me, grasped my hips in his hands and, gorged my slit with his giant erection. My body hanging there, as it were, on his firm pego, he swung me to and fro with ever increasing rapidity, my nipples titillated by friction against the bedclothes, until his balls, which knocked against my belly, gave up the fight and let loose their stores of satisfying sperm.

When I was rested I wanted to go back to my room. "Not yet," he said. And, as he sat on the edge of the bed, he put his head down to my thing and commenced tickling it with his tongue. His extended abdomen was asking my caresses and, bending over, I paid his kisses back to his cock which responded quickly to circling lips and titillating tongue.

"You naughty boy, you want me to eat it up." "Will you?" "I'll do anything you want, and enjoy it as much as you do."

He rolled over on his back, holding his prick and said, "Come." "I'll come, and you will too." And, on my knees over his face, he seized my hips, raised his face to my quim, pressed the edges apart and darted his tongue within.

Rounding up my back so my mouth would reach his prick, and squeezing his balls, I took the red mouthful and sucked—and sucked—we both sucked, until the succulent glands gave up their stores and our breathless bodies lay panting in satisfaction.

CHAPTER XX

When I returned to my room I threw myself on the bed and dropped asleep. Waking late in the afternoon I had barely time to dress and get supper ready for Ralph. As I hurried around I noticed some papers stuck under the door and, picking them up, I found receipts for three months' rent; one for each fuck. Oh, how happy I felt. The crisis had passed and I could lift the care that was worrying Ralph.

It was Friday and I was determined to wait until Sunday before telling him. Worried, as he was, he did not touch me and I said to myself: "Well my fine fellow, that's right, take a rest; store up a good stock of love cream in your testicles. You will want to flood me with it when I relieve your mind with my receipts."

Sunday morning we lay in bed—just awake—and I turned to him, kissed him and passed my hand along his thighs till I felt his cock stiffening in my grasp. "Come, Madge, I'm ashamed of myself for worrying so about this cursed rent. We'll forget it for today, at least, and have a good, old fashioned fuck." And, sitting up in bed he pulled off his night shirt and lying back, held up his stiffened staff ready to stick into me.

"Wait a moment!" and jumping up I ran naked to the closet, got the receipts, handed them to him and stood by the bedside, radiant. "How did you get these?" he cried, and with a glib tongue I told him all. Then he seized me. "You wicked little harlot, you make your room rent by renting your cunt to your landlord, do you?" And, flinging me on the bed he mounted me and plunging his cock full tilt into my ring of love, diddled me until we both lay panting happily.

I was describing my intrigue with the landlord when a knock interrupted me. Opening the door I found our landlord's card—and on the back written: "Will you both join me for dinner, at one o'clock?" "How nice," I cried. "You want to get that big prick of his in you again," said Ralph. "Of course I do," I answered, "and I bet you're dying to see that little dwarf put it in." "Right you are. But Madge, bathe this hard-on in cold water, I want to keep it for afternoon."

I obeyed, and succeeded in wilting it without losing anything. Then, dressing to avoid temptation, we went and breakfasted at a restaurant, and, taking a brisk walk, returned to the house feeling fine and ready to dine and diddle. We met our landlord at the door. "I've told him all," I said, and my tall hubby grasped the hands of the sturdy little new lover.

"Is the dinner to be a full dress affair?" I asked. They both laughed and Ralph answered: "Let's wear nothing except stockings and night shirts." And, going to our rooms we soon looked like two angels ready to ascend, and I guess Ralph was, from the way he stuck out in front.

Slipping downstairs, when no one was around, we found our host ready. I must give him a name; let's call him "Noah"—and laughing at our funny costumes we sat down, eating, drinking, and telling erotic episodes in our lives until the board lost its charm and we were eager for bed.

Raising his glass Noah said: "I drink to the sweetest little cunt I ever tasted. May it always have what it wants as handy as now." Laughing, I arose, slipping the disfiguring gown off my shoulders and standing there nude before them, one knee over the back of my chair—thus opening my slit wide—and, raising my glass: "I drink to man, to the manliest part of him; and then those two dear images of Priapus so near to me. May they ever be ready, with rigid staff and juicy sperm, to carry rapture to any woman's cunt that is as hot as mine is now!" And I drained my glass to the bottom.

Both sprang to their feet, Noah on his chair, and dropping their shirts which hung a moment suspended on their pegos, they emptied their glasses and I was quickly in their arms.

A lascivious group of three, groping and frigging each other, soon stood beside the bed. "After you," said Noah to Ralph. With my dear hubby resting his shoulders on the edge of the bed, his feet on the ground, I straddled over him and could thus rape him standing upright.

"Let me put it in," cried Noah, and, pointing the dear yard straight up, I impaled myself on it and, grasping his buttocks in my hands: "I'll ravish you!" I cried, and commenced to pump up his spermatic treasures with a lubric working bum, while the lustful Noah handled our battling organs and spurred us on with excited speech until my contracting cunny and Noah's frigging fingers drew from Ralph a belly full of seed. He did not wait to have his pego wilt inside of me, but pulled it out still rosy, rampant, and juicy, and drawing himself up flat on the bed, made me take his darling spending cock in my mouth. While from behind me on the floor, the immense pego of the excited clipyard was thrust into my suspended belly. I made my still lustful slit so tight and hard and deep that, when his mighty cock began to throb and spend, I had to let off my own excited emissions and return drop for drop, his vivifying emissions while my lips continued eagerly giving pleasure to Ralph's rosy rooster.

Lying throbbing on the bed they washed me off, gave me and themselves a reviving bumper of wine while Ralph, lighting a cigar, threw himself on a sofa and bade Noah do what he pleased with me. In two minutes his hands had groped and his lips had kissed every part of me and penetrated every cranny.

"What a delicious morsel of flesh she is!" he cried. "What a delicious morsel of flesh this is!" I answered, caressing his stiffened shaft. "It looks ready to inundate my womb again." "It is!" he cried. And jumping up, my short but athletic lover seized me in his arms and standing bolt upright, putting his arms between my legs and grasping a cheek of my buttocks in each hand, he lifted me to a level with his face while I thrust my thighs around his neck, holding his head in my hands to steady myself. His nose just rubbing against my slit, his tongue penetrated it until I squirmed vigorously and he slid my body down along his chest till the stiff spear penetrated my gaping and excited slit. Calling to Ralph to whistle a jig, he danced briskly, while his swelling prick also danced lustfully to my insides and I kept time, with heaving belly and wriggling bottom until languor laid us on our backs on the bed.

"Your belly's too full for this," said Ralph, kneeling over me and holding up his prick in my face. I quickly devoured the tid-bit of raw flesh and washed the draughts of thick cream down with a plentious flow of saliva. "Give me a taste," excitedly exclaimed Noah; and, as I let myself fall back on the pillow the lecherous man with eager lips seized the still foaming spigot and sucked with sodomistic eagerness the last sperm drops from Ralph's succulent prick.

"Are you disgusted?" asked Noah, as he drank a glass of wine. "I haven't done such a thing in twenty years. Away back when I had the mining fever, we were snowed in one winter, six of us men, in one house way up in the mountains. We couldn't get out and time went slowly. One day, as we had just finished dining and each of us had three or four drinks of whiskey in us, we discovered written in soot over the fireplace: 'Boys, let's suck each other's cocks.' We all looked at each other—who wrote it? All looked innocent when the rough but jolly leader spoke up: 'Boys I didn't write it but, damn it, it's set me thinking. I bet there is not a mother's son of you here who don't jerk himself off on the sly.'

"Then opening his breeches he pulled out his stiff prick. 'I'll suck any of you who will suck this.' Our pretended virtue melted away, and the rest of us eagerly produced our peckers. In a minute we divided into three couples and each of our mouths were full of fine erections and we were swallowing sperm at one end and spitting it at the other."

This story, though vile according to our education, excited me and I threw myself between Noah's thighs and kissed his prick. Quickly grasping my buttocks he pulled them up to his head and plunging his tongue into my slit we both started on a sucking race, while Ralph, seizing a limber cane, tingled our heaving backsides with a rapid flogging.

CHAPTER XXI

The next morning when I got out of bed, long after Ralph had left, I found three letters under the door. The first was from Noah and contained a hundred dollar bill. "Don't refuse this, dear girl, fifty thousand dollars wouldn't repay the pleasures I have tasted."

The second was from my dear John and enclosed an introduction for Ralph to an old friend in New York. John wrote that his friend, Phillip Weston, was wealthy and might find Ralph more lucrative employment. Then he wrote tenderly and amorously about his thinking of me, and turning the page I read, "Yes, my dear girl, as I sit here the thought of you sends a vigorous thrill through my shaft. I hold it in my hand wishing it in yours, or your plump bubbies, eager mouth, tight cul or sweet and luscious cunt. I lay it against the paper and trace it thus (here an outline of his prick) and now I fold the paper around it and frig into it the sperm your image raises." All over the inside of the sheet were blotches of brown stuff that had been hot, rich cream, gushing from his dear pego. Opening my thighs I pressed the paper deep into my lustful crevice and, rubbing it and dreaming that his dear form was naked in my arms—I, too, wet the paper and laid it aside to dry and send back to him.

The third letter was in a strange hand and,

as I opened it, another hundred dollar bill dropped out. "A slight memento my dear girl, of a delightful day in a parlor car." No signature, but I knew that it was from that railroad director who let us into his private room and who I took into my private parts.

"Two hundred dollars," I soliloquized, and, lifting up my thighs in the air I held them wide apart and gazed into the opening of my red crevice—"Two hundred dollars just because you were nice to two men. Ah, if you were paid at that rate every time you sucked the delightful overflow out of your frisky guests, your owner would be a millionaire by this time."

A key turned in the lock and Ralph entered. He burst out laughing. "Don't stir, you're an awful smutty picture." "The picture is at your service," I answered, hugging my legs closely down to the sides of my body, my feet at the side of my head. "Keep that position," he cried, pulling my wide-stretched buttocks to the edge of the bed and, placing my shoulders high on the pillows, devoured the lustful attitude for a minute. "I'm going to suck you first, fuck you second, and then suck you again and, if you get out of that position before I get through, I won't diddle you for a week." "Hurry up then, I'm ready to spend now." And his tongue was thrust into my cunt, stretched wider than ever before and brought down my ready juices almost immediately. "Don't budge except to heave your ass," he cried and, into my still lustful slit he drove his excited penis, quickly sending the blissful balm to the inner parts to solace my lecherous agony, and, again on his knees, he kept his tongue working in my cunt and trust a finger in my cul until I could stand it no longer and cried out that he would kill me if he kept on.

Then throwing himself on the bed, he made me fondle his prick and buttocks while he read the letters. Later, after a smoke with the landlord, he came up and said they were going to a theater and, as I said good-bye to them at the door, the air seemed so fresh and invigorating that, though it was dark, I determined to take a walk.

Sauntering along looking into shop windows, I came into a side street which I afterwards found out was a cruising ground for women of pleasure. Presently a rough grasp on my shoulder startled me, and, looking up, I saw it was a big, burly policeman.

"What are you cruising for, don't you get enough cocks staying in the house? Don't you know it's against the law?" I was too frightened to answer. "By Jove, you're a new girl in these sections," he continued, "and a damned nice looking one. Come into the alley and let me see if the rest of you is as nice as your face." And he dragged me along a dark narrow street. "Please let me go!" I cried. "You will either come with me or I will run you into the station," he said. And, pulling me along the deserted alley we came to where a solitary lamp threw a flood of light down on a wagon. The powerful rascal seized me and threw me on my back on the tail board of the cart, my legs hanging down. "Pull up your petticoats!" he ordered, "I've no time to waste. The sergeant will be around shortly and will give me hell if he catches me off my post. See—I've got a good stiff-on." And I saw his magnificent prick erect against his belly. It's the quickest way to get out of the scrape, I thought, and, pulling my clothes up to the pit of my stomach, I awaited his attack. "Jolly, you're a daisy," he said, passing his rough hand over thigh and belly and gave my brush a squeeze that made me wince.

"In it goes," he cried. "How's that for a stretcher?" I tried to keep still, but his big prick and splendid stroking made me forget all but the pleasure of his thrusts and I had to work my bottom. "Oh, you like it, do you? You needn't deny it. I know when a girl shams and when she is tickled in the right spot." And working harder, I gave myself up to it and cried out: "It's lovely. Your splendid cock is making me spend." "So you shall, my dear," and his colossal prick, knocking at my womb, shot its flood of lust into my cunt, sweltering in its own overflow.

"I've caught you, have I?" said a voice out of the shadow. "Fucking a whore in the public streets and off your post." And the speaker, another big policeman, stood looking down at our exposed lechery.

"Ah, now, Sergeant, what's the harm of diddling a gal? It don't take long. And Sergeant, look at her. She's a new one. See what a fine pair of legs and how her belly heaves; and her slit's as hot as a slut's. She gives a stroke up for every one down. Try her, Sergeant." And, standing aside, he put his hands under my bottom and lifted me up to give his superior a better view of my venereal attractions.

The sergeant stepped between my legs. "Well my dear, I don't want to be hard on your lover, so I'll be hard on you instead." And, in an instant his splendid cock was plunged into me and another splendid diddle made me squirm. "Meet us here again tomorrow night," said the Sergeant, "and don't come out of the alley till we are out of sight."

When I did come out I was not long in getting home. I remember to this day the sensations of shame and fear I experienced that evening, but I also remember the uncontrollable pleasure those two police cocks, as big as their clubs, gave me on the wagon in the alley.

CHAPTER XXII

It took me an hour to recover from the effects of the unexpected charge of the blue coated pair of lusty baton wielders. But I could not, despite the ignominy of having myself thus stormed and barebellied in the public street, be unconscious of the full fledged, firm fixed, fine fucking faculties of my last lovers. And my feverish, yes, ferocious fuck funnel forced me to feel the folly of feeling foolish over this fortuitous fornication, and set my brain to work to plan some new deviltry; with my cunt as the center of the celebration.

"I have it. I'll disguise myself and solicit Ralph and Noah on their way home."

Donning some old clothes which I never wore, I again sallied forth at about the time the theater was out and walked along the way I knew they would return.

I hadn't gone a block when two young fellows came along. "Well sweetest," said one, "are you looking for a tenant who'll move in your empty room, stay a while, dance a jig, and then vacate? By Jove, Jack. She ain't bad. Damn the cost. Let's take her to Mother Jones' for a short razzle dazzle."

"Go away and leave me along!" I said. "Leave you alone and unprotected? Oh, no," said the youngster. "Come along," and each seized an arm. "Where are you taking me?"

I cried. "To bed," said one, and around a corner we went and up to a door. "Here Mother, here's your dollar. Which room?" "Is it for one jerk, or for the night?" said the buxom landlady. "Oh, only a lightning thrust," one answered. "Then come into my room," she said, and into a room we went. "Pay her," said the Madam, and the youngsters handed me a bill which I put into my pocket, and, in a jiffy, I was on the bed with a nice, young cock working in me. Then, fire, bang, and another was promenading in my Rue-Rogue. "She'll do," cried one. "She's bully," said the other. "We'll make it longer next time." And they were gone.

Fifteen minutes had hardly elapsed from start to finish. "Well, my dear," said the woman, "that's quick work. If all your lovers take so little of your time you'll get rich quick. Clean up and take another stroll and you may land some more fish. The theaters are just letting out and I bet you will be back with a new stiff in an hour."

I didn't answer. The word "theater" brought me back to what I had started for. So I left hastily to look for Ralph and Noah. Several men accosted me but I said that I was engaged.

Presently my old "long and short of it" hove in sight. "What a funny pair," I said, laughing at their faces. "You'll make fun of us, will you?" said Ralph, and he began groping me. "There's nothing like novelty," he continued, "and my pego was stiff as soon as she hove in sight. Let's take her to your room for a brace of jerks. The other one will be asleep."

So done, and into Noah's room we went, and when the gas was turned on there was a tableau. I took off my bonnet and they recognized me. I burst with a hearty laugh. "I'll stop your laughing!" said Ralph, and, throwing me back on the sofa, he stuck his prick in my mouth for a stop cock, while my slit had another, of Noah's flesh.

One evening Ralph came home: "Madge, I am going to leave for several days; not a word—I can't explain now. Noah will be your guardian meanwhile. Come help me pack." As I packed I watched him bathe, till finishing he turned and said: "Now for a farewell fuck." In an instant I was on the bed with his dear form, almost in tears, but teeming with voluptuous rapture. Finished, he dressed and took me to Noah, and explained: "Noah, you will play protector to her and see she doesn't want for anything. A field not ploughed and watered soon grows stale. Harrow her well; plough her frequently and irrigate her freely. I won't be jealous if you show her the lively sight of the city. Let her see and feel all she can, for it may be that my journey will result in our leaving New York and settling elsewhere." He clasped me in his arms and was gone.

After I had sobbed for a time, I jumped on Noah's lap and felt something hard pressing my bottom. "Oh, you dear fellow, you want to commence being husband right off." "Not now. Go and get that letter on the desk." I got it and handed it to him. "Go sit on that chair for I can't stand the warmth of your body; and I want to keep fresh for tonight."

"What's up tonight?" "Lots of things will be up," and opening the letter—"this is from a tenant of mine. She keeps a house of high-toned lechery. Runs the full gamut of lustful sights and sensations. And it is an invitation to be present at a soiree tonight. It's not an ordinary house of pleasure, but where experts jaded with the everyday experiences in sexual matters, have provided for them a select show of sometimes outrageous novelties. She is a woman of originality and one who goes to these carnal sprees must obey her and furnish their share of pleasure by giving themselves freely to anything her fancy dictates. Will you go?"

"I have never been in such a crowd. My hot thoughts imagine such things, but—if you like I will go." "Good. Now go to your room and sleep until I call you." "What shall I wear?" "Your prettiest pair of stockings—and a waterproof coat to cover you till we get there. We will go in a carriage, and mind, no finger fumbling in the meantime."

I did not awake until Noah knocked. Jumping up I put on a pair of black silk stockings, which Noah gartered halfway up my thighs. "Now slippers and coat; see, I am Adam in a hustler." So costumed we were rapidly driven away.

It was a fine house. A darky in livery admitted us and directed us to our "undressing" rooms. In mine I found three pretty nudes arranging hair, stockings, etc. "Ah, here's number four. We are waiting for you, hurry up and get your working clothes like ours." As I stripped the three girls embraced me. "Well, I guess we're up to concert pitch," said one, as a large, fine looking woman entered with nothing on but a huge rubber dildo hanging from a chain around ner neck.

"I guess I know all of you," she said, "except

this one," coming to me and grasping my hairy hole. "Kiss this emblem of Priapus, my dear?" As I took it in my mouth she squeezed the syringe and shot a white liquid into it. They all laughed and we followed the Madam into a bright, lighter room.

Facing us were eight men in line, Noah on a stool. We lined facing them. "Show them your cunts." Leaning back we opened the lips of our ruby cock suckers to expose the ruby interiors. "Fuck each mouth with your tongue and frig their pricks!" I saw her tongue in the first fellow's mouth and his cock in her hand, and we all followed. Delicious! Think of having eight different pegos in your hand in two minutes.

"All on your backs with legs wide apart!" Men opposite women, we gloated over each other's secret gifts.

"I'll call you by number. Cock one and cunt four will hand frig!" One of the girls and one of the men ran to the couch and, head to foot, grasped prick and slit, and frigged. The girl squirmed and his sperm shot high in the air.

"Cock two, rape cunt three!" The girl ran around the room, the stiff cocked man after her—with a sudden rush he seized her, flung her on the couch and ravished her.

"Cock three in the backside of cunt two!" This was Noah. The pretty girl, with her bum high in the air, was plugged by his big prick, while with fine stroking he tickled her in front.

"Cock four and cunt one!" This was me. "Put cunt on the edge!" and I lay, with legs wide apart on the edge of the couch. "First in mouth, then in bubbies, then in cunt, then suck each other!" In a second my fine stallion thrust his big prick between my lips and I grasped it with them a moment. Then he moved back and I held my breasts firmly around it while he worked. A moment later the excited pego was plunged to the hilt in my belly and gave me a dozen lovely jerks, but, feeling the end approaching he pulled it out and, as I rolled on my side, stuck his head between my thighs and his tongue into my slit while I eagerly took his firm prick in my mouth and sucked it dry. Spend? I should say I did, and I sucked so much sperm into my belly as to keep me from hunger for a day.

I can't tell all. Each coupling was different.

My second lover stood upright on the couch, I resting on my elbows, my body in the air, and plugged me from behind.

After a volley or two from each, we rested, the men with their cigars and us with cigarettes. A pretty, naked, little boy and girl, just adolescent, served us with wine. The men played with the girl's slit and the women with the boy's pintle till he could stand it no longer. Cupid seized his Psyche and pulled her, playing prude, to the couch, where, flat on her back and he on her belly, we had the delight of watching these two working their fresh thighs in blissful ardor. Then Madam said: "It's time I take a turn. Sam!" and another black Sam, like mine, with a cock straight in the air, ran in, seized the buxom woman, tumbled her on the couch and poured in her a volley of thrusts that shook her fat body, then drew out his pego and they sucked each other dry.

Seating herself, still wriggling, she said: "Now I have a novelty for you. Within five minutes you will see a woman's maidenhead taken before your eyes." Going out she returned, leading in one hand a girl of sixteen and with the other a young fellow of twenty, both naked and well shaped.

"This couple wanted to marry, but couldn't afford to furnish rooms for themselves. I offered to do it if they would do their first belly-pumping for your delectation." And turning to the bridegroom, "Go and show the gentlemen your bride's a virgin!" And the fellow seized the girl and soon all those old rogues were groping her virgin slit. "Oh, oh, I can't stand it, I'm on fire!" and taking her in his arms her groom threw her on the edge of the couch and put his prick into her virgin cunt. "Oh, it hurts!" she cried—but he couldn't stop; he seized her bottom and drove into her. What a delightful sight. A virgin squirming and spitting on a hot poker! She writhed and wriggled, but the stiff standard still forced its way and, finally, driven in to the hilt, she shrieked aloud until the healing balm shot for the first time into her ruptured slit.

As the knocked out hymen breaker withdrew, one of the men shouted to him, "I'll give you fifty dollars to let me fuck her—just as she lies." "Done!" answered the lover, and the newly opened cunt soon had his big prick stretching its narrow sides and the wriggling buttocks showed that she began to feel that there was some fun in the work—as well as hurt—for when he withdrew the girl rolled over on the couch squirming.

"Fifty dollars to take this," cried another, jumping up cock in hand. "Done," again said the mercenary husband, and the new bidder rolled the panting girl on her back and flat on her belly gave her a vigorous diddle.

As he arose—"That will do," said Madam. "You'll kill the girl," and, turning to the husband, "Keep those other men out of her by sticking your own prick in and carrying her out, spitted on it." And the fellow pierced her and ran out with her, working in her belly as he went.

The scene had worked us all up. "Girls, stand up in the middle of the room!" and we grouped ourselves together. Suddenly all was darkness; we shrieked when Madam called out: "Go for them boys! Do anything you like in the dark!"

What happened I can't describe but must leave to your imagination. Think of four naked girls and eight naked men, all wild with lust, rolling and writhing in a heap on the floor; one minute a man's hand was on my cunt; the next a plump bottom rubbed against my face; then a tongue was thrust into my slit and a cock was rubbing against the cheeks of my buttocks; again, a man fell flat, full length upon me and we rolled over and over together; another man tore me away and standing, pushed me down on his prick. "Suck it!" I grabbed his thighs in my arms and his cock in my mouth, when I felt my buttocks raised higher up and another stiff staff stuck into my cunt from behind and I hung, suspended thus, when the room was re-illuminated.

"Hello! here's a new kink," and those who had finished their shot gathered around our group and watched me in the lustful agony of sucking sperm into me at both ends at once.

We all arose, went into another room and

plunged into a tank of heated water until, refreshed, we jumped out and rubbed each other down, paying special attention to the carnal parts whose lusts we were reviving. Then to the dining room where a luscious but light lunch and oceans of champagne mingled with smutty talk and touches, kindled our fires anew.

"Let's have a song," said Madam, and she called upon one of the girls, who, rising and going through a smutty pantomine with fingers and slit, sang:

Though I eat and drink and dress,
I am frank and will confess
I'm not satisfied with less
Than a good hot diddle, in my middle.

Though I like a squeezing hand
And a good hot hug can stand,
I'd rather much to land
With a good cock, that is red—on a bed.

I'm not virtuous a bit,
I live but for my slit,
If you've a prick you think will fit
Stick it in—to my quim.

I've tried big ones and tried little,
I've been frigged, fucked and diddled
With your pego, always pickle,
I'm a whore—to the core.

It's not bad—is it? there,
Gaping red in curly hair.
Come, walk into my lair,
With your prick—fuck me quick.

You may grope me hard all over
O'er breast and bum be rover,
But you'll never be in clover
Till your hunt ends—in my cunt.

It is hot and it is juicy,
So come and do your duty,
Ah, your cock it is a beauty,
Put it slam—in my clam.

If you're feeble and played out,
Or a lazy, flabby lout,
I'll wabble it about
Till it stands—if I can.

But if you want a kiss,
From your pego loving Miss
To make you feel the bliss
Of a stand—in my hand.

I will tongue, taste and tickle,
Nor e'en at sucking stickle,
But, in my mouth will pickle
Your staff—till you laugh.

I've got a good hot mate,
He can take me crooked, straight,
And can even try his fate
In my bum—till he come.

Ah, I'm so fond of sperm,
Spouting from a prick that's firm,
Seeing only makes me squirm,
Feeling makes me work—with a jerk.

I can take—gents—all you've got,
Whether one or a whole lot.

I'm a hot, sperm guzzled sot.
Come and rut—in my gut.

Never yet have I had enough
Of stiff prick and creamy stuff,
And I won't give you a bluff
But will spend—when you spend.

Oh, how sweet it is to diddle
With cock and balls to fiddle,
Put the stiff—into your middle
Deep stuck—then fuck.

So, whenever you want fucking,
Whipping, rubbing, frigging, sucking,
Remember—at cock working
I'm no slouch—on a couch.

We all applauded the singer, and the lusty fellow at her side seized her leg and, straddling her over him, threw her flat on her back on the table. Then rising, he fucked her there, right before our eyes. She was no sooner seated in her chair than one of the fellows called for a fresh bottle of champagne and, seizing the lively girl, laid her on the table in front of him. Taking the bottle he uncorked it and plunged the fizzing neck into her slit, tipping it up until she overflowed with wine and, removing the bottle, he sucked it out of her.

Then the fellow at my right sprang to his feet, his cock sticking out over the table. "Jerk it off," he cried, and I frigged it till the sperm flew high across the table and the girl opposite tried to take it in a goblet, mouth and slit; then he made me finish by taking it in my mouth.

This kept up till we were half tipsy, and returning to the parlor, lay around in the wildest abandon waiting for anything that might happen.

A middle aged man came in with a boy of eighteen, both dressed. "Ah, my boy, do you ever play with this?" And the older fellow began squeezing the boy's navel. "Ah, it's getting stiff. Don't you wish that I was a nice pretty girl and would lift up my clothes and let you play with my cunt, and then give this stiff little cock a fuck in it? Ah, my boy, we can have fun, too," (and unbuttoning the boy's trousers his erection was in his grasp). "Oh, how pretty it looks!" And kneeling before the object of his lust, the old lecherer fondled his victim's cock and played with his balls until, with a cry of gloating lechery, he took the swollen penis in his mouth and sucked it—the boy calling out to him to suck harder and showing plainly how he enjoyed the spending.

Wild with his sodomistic passion the sucker seized his prey, turned him on his belly and pulled his bottom. Then, flat on his back, he drew the boy's tight cul, while with his hand he frigged the boy's cock until he had sent his sperm into his bottom. Then, flat on his back, he drew the boy on top of him and with his lustful mouth sucked dry the fresh, young pintle.

No sooner had they left the scene when two robust black men, weighing at least two hundred pounds apiece, came in. "Jolly Sambo, I just saw a sight that made my prick as stiff as a poker. I was passing Massa' bedroom and I heard Missus cry out: 'Oh go away, you ought to be ashamed. Wait till we get to bed.' 'Does that look as though I could wait?' And I looked over the door and saw Massa strip himself, then tear off pretty Missus' clothes and, throwing her on the bed, diddle her well. Come on, Sambo, let's strip and have a suck."

Quickly the two big blacks were stark naked and in an instant, rolling on the couch, the two lustful mouths seized each other's immense pricks and we had the exciting sight of those two muscular giants sucking like mad at one another's spigots. When they broke away, Madame cried: "Ladies number one and four will go stiffen and fuck those black giants!" This was me, and number four was about my size, we evidently having been selected as a contrast to our negro lovers, being the smallest women in the room.

"Come on," cried my excited companion, and in an instant we were in the arms of our African partners. Lord! how they mauled us—now a finger, now a tongue in my slit, now my black lover on top of me, then I on him, then, stooping us both over, they worked their cocks in unison between our buttocks. Then, lying us side by side on our backs, they stood between our legs and we saw their terrifying cocks as big as when they had first entered. "Oh!" I shrieked, "I can't stand it," and, seizing the immense erection, my slit was feasted with a royal prick giving it a royal fuck.

"Change partners," and the black tackled me, put his tongue into me. I, mad with lust, seized the drooping but swollen monster, frigged it in my hands, rubbed it against my bubbies—"Kiss it, you whore." And I kissed and sucked till he seized me, threw himself on his back, pulled my slit to his face and fucked it with his tongue while I eagerly seized his throbbing cock in my mouth and tongue-tickled and sucked till the sperm strangled me. Then the lusty black, reversing his position, threw himself flat on my belly and thrust his volcanic cock deep into my cunt—working at me till I lay panting and exhausted and the two blacks, jumping to their feet, looked down gloatingly on us two willing victims of their lechery while the crowd clapped their hands and cried "Bravo!"

CHAPTER XXIII

But I must not keep on—a woman's cunt is the true perpetual motion. At least mine has never stopped, and to tell you of all its quests, and guests, and how they made themselves at home in it, would take a book as big as the Bible.

The next day, Noah said that a turkish bath would be the best thing to rejuvenate us and that he knew a quiet, small one where a man and a woman could take one together.

As he paid the female keeper he was asked which rubber he wanted, and answered that he wanted the strongest. "He's black," said the keeper. "Oh, we don't mind that."

Soon we were in a room as hot as my disposition, perspiring and naked, then sponged with cold water and plunged in a cool pool. I forgot all the processes which we went through alone. "Now for the rubbing," and entering the room, we found our black manipulator awaiting us, a naked giant with a girdle around his loins. We had sheets thrown around us and Noah, dropping his, threw himself flat on a leather cot and the Negro commenced working his muscles, limbering his joints and rubbing him all over with the palms of his hands.

"Ah, Madge, that puts new life into me," said Noah, as I watched the process. "I should smile," said the smiling black; and he held up

Noah's prick strutting perpendicularly. "It feels as if he wanted something sweeter Miss."

Throwing aside my sheet I told the black to lift me up on top of Noah, and I was quickly taking the starch out of him. As I lay with his prick dissolved inside of me: "Do you want to pump sperm into her?" asked Noah of the black. "Let's see your cock," and the lustful black stripped off the girdle and Noah and I had the brown and red sceptre in our grasp.

"Run," said Noah, pushing me off the side opposite the black. I ran around the room, the black after me, until, rushing to Noah, he placed me on top of him; my belly over his face. As I took his prick in my mouth, the lustful black cock was guided by Noah into my slit and the God-like thrusts soon carried rapture through me and drowned my vitals in burning sperm while I gratified Noah with a hot-mouthed sucking.

Then we all took a plunge in the bath again and, coming out, "Put the girdle on," Noah said, "so as not to tempt this young filly again."

"No, no, I must have one more taste of this delicious prick," and throwing myself on my knees before the colored giant, I caressed with hands, titties and mouth the already magnificent erection of his God-like cunt plough.

"You'll promise to quit with one more fuck?" "I swear!" I cried. And, kneeling on the couch, Noah leaned my back against his breast, my bum on the edge of the bed. He bade the black lift me up by the legs and, grasping them, he pulled them on each side of my shoulders, leaving my slit a gaping furnace with the doors wide open.

"What a fine view," cried the Negro, dropping to his knees, and he not only viewed, but stuck his tongue into the stretched orifice. "Stop, you'll make me spend," I cried. "So I will, Miss," and, on his feet, he quickly drove his big prick to the hair in my cunt and fucked me until I squealed.

Two days later I was alone when a lady called. She was about my size and age; except she was a blonde and I was a brunette. She handed me a card—Mrs. Philip Weston. "Oh, yes, John had sent Ralph an introduction to Philip Weston—but we learned that he was away from the city."

"Yes, your Uncle John wrote about you, but we have not been here since we received the letter." She seated herself by my side. "We'll be friends, shan't we?" I kissed her and she went on: "Philip is away, but next week we sail south on our yacht. John, knowing that we're to be with him for a visit sent you this letter," handing it to me.

"Dear Madge—It's no use. I can't live here without you and Ralph. I have written him to give up his position and for you and him to settle here with me, as the sole heirs of all I possess. You can come on with Mr. and Mrs. Weston."

"Oh, how splendid," I cried, gladly. "And are you and John well acquainted?" I asked. "That's a pointed question," she laughed, "but I know all about your relations with John and he knows as much about me as Philip does. We're both lewd, lustful women, and I'm not ashamed of it! Are you?" "I live only for sexual enjoyment," I answered.

"Let's strip and have our first embrace," she cried. And soon a naked blonde and brunette were admiring, caressing, praising the charms of each other and, quickly on the bed, sought, with experienced tongues to quench the lustful fires that for the moment no man's pego was there to put out.

I told her of Noah—"How funny to have a dwarf for a lover." "You'll have one in a minute." I ran downstairs and, finding him, quickly told him, while I handled his prick: "Strip here, clothes will only be in the way," and in five minutes I introduced my lover to Mary.

Putting her on my lap, "Come, Noah, and examine her," and my dear lover was on his knees, kissing and tickling her swelling belly and luscious cunt, which she jutted out for him.

"Stop," she cried, "let me feel and kiss that big prick before you fuck me." Kneeling over her, she soon had a mouth full of stiff prick and a handful of red balls.

"Quick, diddle me. I'm consumed with lechery," she said, throwing herself back with extended thighs, and as he stuck his flaming nozzle to her door I guided it in.

How that woman loved it. How she heaved her belly, threw up her legs, pounded with her hands his bare bum, till on the verge of the precipice. "Now, shoot it into me, I'm coming." As I knelt beside the lustful warrior, the big prick swelled larger and larger. "Ouch! there it comes. It's shooting all through me! Oh, your lovely cock! Your delicious fucking! Give me every drop!" In a moment she lay heaving.

My cunt hot? I should say it was. I was flat on my back, my fingers clutching it. "Stop! give her a taste of your tongue," and Noah was in a moment sucking my slit, while she stuck her tongue in my mouth till I overflowed.

We did not separate till exhausted. Mary arranged to have me join her and Philip a week later in Philadelphia.

One evening Noah entertained three of his friends.

After they got lively he came and told me his friends were in a mood to appreciate a female friend, which he told them he would furnish if they would appear as Adam.

He led me naked into his room and introduced me to three fine, stalwart clipyards. And, within fifteen minutes I had been well fucked by four cocks, and lay panting with the sperm oozing out of my slit.

Before Noah carried me to my room, twelve shots had been fired into my various holes.

CHAPTER XXIV

All my attention was devoted to Noah the last week, and, when I said good-bye to him he talked more like a father than a lover, and gave me a certificate of deposit for two thousand dollars. "Something for a rainy day," he said.

Arriving at Philadelphia, I soon had Mary in my arms. "Come to my room. For one night one room will do for the three of us, won't it?"

After a bath, she put her arms around me. "Now dear, I'll introduce you to my husband." Out from behind the window curtains stepped Philip Weston, stark naked, his rosy rooster ready to ravish me. Grabbing my arms she held them behind my back. "Come examine this new cock cooler." "Cock cooler! The mere sight of it burns me up." And, his hands and kisses covered me, then led me to the bed. His wife pointed his robust cock at my slit and, with a heave, he was in to the hilt.

The first fuck is always nice, and we played with agile loins until drained of our bliss. Two more rounds, then, for the night he slept sandwiched between two warm specimens of woman flesh.

The next afternoon we boarded the yacht and were off for our long sail. The crew consisted of three big Italians and a Chinese cook who kept to the galley unless called for.

After land disappeared, Mary said: "Come Madge, let's get into our high-sea rig."

We were stripped to our stockings and were just reaching for our sailor suits when a voice from the doorway said, "Missy, Captain Phil sent a bottle of wine." "Come in, Ah Wing," and the cook entered in a blue blouse reaching to his knees, and served the wine as we lay stretched naked on the divan. "Ah Wing, how's this for a pretty tickler?" as she raised one of my legs, showing my fucking facilities.

"Ah Wing, show the lady what a Chinese cock looks like," and pulling his blouse over his head, stepped naked to the edge of the divan, and I had a Chinese prick in my hand for the first time. Long, and the end of it curved like a finger with the top joint bent, it was smaller around than a white man's, with a crisp little pair of balls, no bigger than a large dog's.

"Let Chinee-man kiss cunny," and his tongue shot into my slit, when springing up: "Me allee ready fuckee," and I pointed his long, slim cock at my crevice and its curved end was soon tickling the instrument of joy. "Ah, I see why you like the heathen fucking! Don't tickle the itching; Ah Wing will make me say ah-ah-ah in a second," and he did.

Our sea clothes: our red jackets exposed our breasts at every flop, and a pair of pants in two pieces, only connected by the waistband, leaving our mounts exposed when we opened our legs, and when we stooped our bare bottom was exposed fully. "Come on deck, I bet there is a quartet of stiff pricks ready to sing to us."

All in line, with Phil in command, the four

muscular men were stark naked, with stiff pricks, waiting for us.

This is your initiation on board the *San Sousiand,* you must take the whole four of these shots into your pretty cunt," and they threw me on one of the cushioned seats and, opening my legs, my belly and slit lay open to their lust.

I got soundly fucked by four pricks—one after the other, either of which would make a girl heave her belly, throw up her legs and spend! My cunt was as full as an ocean of water; I panted, writhed like a worm, and with glad ears drank in their words of appreciation as they shot into me their spermy fluid.

I lay, with legs fallen apart, panting breasts, heaving belly, and gaping slit; Mary hugging, kissing and congratulating me, until she saw the Chinaman leering at us from the galley. Springing up she rolled on her back at my side, opened wide her thighs and, that long slim cane was soon scratching the red and itching interior of her crevice.

A week of this; living around loose, and exchanging with each other every form of licentious lust—to describe it would be endless. I must turn to the last chapter, of our welcome at Beauvoir.

CHAPTER XXV

We sailed up the Mississippi to as near Beauvoir as we could, and Mary, Phil and I rode to the hermitage of my desires. Peeping through the window, we beheld John and Ralph reading in the library. I undressed entirely, then ran into the house and stood, eagerly happy, before my darling lovers.

Wild with delight and mad to enjoy me, I denied them until, as naked as myself, first Ralph, then John, with firm, fierce, frenzied pricks, fucked me frantically.

I threw myself on their dear fallen spears and with lewd, loving lips and tongue, brought them to life again. Then Mary and Phil came bounding through the window, where they had watched the first shots fired, and faced us, naked.

"Now I'll introduce you to my husband, as you did to yours," and guiding Ralph's prick into her, we watched these lusty lovers taste for the first time the sweets of cock and cunt.

Then, John quickly sprang into her saddle and her husband into mine and our jockeys, riding gallantly, our bellys were soon inundated at the first finish of frenzied fucking.

Glancing through the window I spied Sam. I darted out and threw myself in his arms. "Strip, quick, and carry me into the house on your prick." And, in a minute, his staff was deep in my belly and, running full tilt, he entered the house and fucked me before the whole company. I squirmed off my still stuck-up slit-sticker and, turning it to Mary's face: "Kiss it—suck it—make it firm again, so he can give your slit a creamy womb opener."

With her labial touches, his prick with stiffened, swelling glands filled her mouth and, grabbing her, he threw her on her back and fucked her into a spasm of spending.

In the doorway appeared my darling Meg, and I led her in, and tearing off her clothes, I turned to Phil: "Isn't she pretty? Brown Venus!" "Splendid!" and quickly his hands and lips fired her at every touch. "My slit's on fire—seething," she cried, and on the couch he gave her a fervent fuck.

We supped naked, each of us drinking a full bottle of champagne. In a dancing, prancing, devil-may-care stage of intoxication, we seven naked, in a group of writhing bodies close together, staggered and reeled into the parlor. And all in a bunch, topsy-turvy, kneeling, lying down, cocks in cunts, in culs, in titties, mouths and hands, we went off together and were flooded, inside and out, with showers of sperm, faces and forms glistening with the shiny emissions and cocks, cunts and mouths covered with the exuberant overflow.

I was too far gone to watch the others. I know that one of the fellows' whiskered mouths was kissing my bottom, thighs and belly and opening my slit. A languid tongue was licking the ruby interior while a fallen prick was six inches from my face. I took it in my mouth and rolled my tongue over it, pulling the hair with my teeth and, taking the crumpled skin in my mouth feasted upon the pearly drops that still oozed from it. John attempted to go out to make water, but Mary took his flabby prick in her mouth and, I could see by the motions of her throat she was swallowing his come. Strangling, she jumped up, shouting, "Oh, it makes me want to come, too." John putting his head in her slit cried, "Come, then!"

Jumping to his feet he seized the shameless Mary, holding the big thighs wide open and, putting her cunt on Sam's big prick, wrapped her legs around his waist. Pushing his cock out for me to wet, he took it out of my mouth and pointed it at Mary's bum, entered it, and the delighted girl screamed with pleasure. Fucking briskly, each cock plunged in and out at the same time, then giving out screams of overwrought excitement, she received the streams from both cocks. And, as her stallions fell exhausted on the floor, she threw herself on top of them and seemed to be eating up their fallen pricks.

The other two men rushed to me and, one in my cunt and one in my mouth, flooded me with sperm and rapture.

Sam, stooping down, put his arms between our legs and, lifting us up, forked thus, and off with us to our room, where he bathed us, laid us in bed as each pressed a good-night kiss on his pego and he on our slits.

CHAPTER XXVI

But, dear Jack, I must stop somewhere, and it shall be with this chapter.

The men arranged a fishing trip and we, poor girls, were left vacant. While lamenting our luck, I heard the gate open, and looking out saw the priest who had married us, coming up the walk.

Laying Mary flat on her back on the sofa I opened the front of her dress to expose her bubbies and, raising one knee, pulled her skirts up so that, by stooping, he could get a full view of her coral cavity. Then I hid myself behind a curtain.

When no one responded to his knock he walked to the piazza and finding the shutters were open he walked in.

Mary's form caught his eye and in a minute he was kneeling at her side: "Holy Virgin, what a pretty prick pleaser," he muttered, but as he looked closer, "That isn't the girl I fucked on her wedding night: it might be the other fellow's wife." He gently lifted her skirts, and, as if moving in her sleep, she let her legs drop wide open and he had the whole kingdom of heaven exposed to him. Jumping up he took out his monster, then knelt between her legs, lifting them up, the true cross which women love to bear was quickly stored away in her innermost sanctuary.

"Oh, I can't play asleep! It's too heavenly! Fuck harder if you'd save me from eternal regrets. Come, Madge, and see this royal priest's relic giving my cunt a sample of the church's creamy charity. As fast as you like, father, I'm ready."

As I watched the charming cunt and colossal cock charging at each other with such rapidity, I grew dizzy and fell back on the floor.

In a minute the priest's sperm-spouting prick was relieving me of my rich store of oily oblation as Mary knelt beside us and squeezed the balm out of his buttocks.

He did not leave us till all our holes had hotly held his fresh and fecundatious prick. When he left, a pecker pronely pulseless, or testicles more wholly empty, could not be found in the buttock wagging world.

Walking along the brook the next day, we heard, "Mine's bigger than yours—I bet I can shoot it further than you!" and we looked down on two little colored boys finishing their bath, and playing with their stiff little cocks.

"They'll waste it if we don't hurry," said Mary. "You naughty boys, aren't you ashamed to play with those things! They don't belong to you at all, but are for the girls." And pulling me beside her, she dragged my skirts to my waist, and I did the same to her. We soon had their pretty little pricks plugging us, to the delight of the four. Then we let them examine us and they were soon again deep in our slits.

When we continued our walk we came upon a black man slouching along. It was the buggerer. He stood still and I saw his lustful eyes on our trim figures, and I knew he was thinking how easy it would be to rape us both.

I walked up to him. "Do you remember me?" He looked doubtful. "I've seen you, Miss, but ain't placed you." Then—"Hell," he cried. "This tells me," and he pulled out his monstrous cock. "I fucked you a year ago." And in two minutes I was fucked again.

"Oh," cried Mary, "help," and she grasped her burning slit. But the black, grabbing one of us in each arm, carried us, running, to his hut and threw us on the same grassy mound my rump had pressed a year before.

Another black, naked, appeared at the door. "Hurry, Bob, I've fucked one and the other wants it bad!" And, as the lust-burned girl opened her legs, the twin of the last erection was plunged, and lunged into a hole hot enough to turn an anchorite into a satyr. And, the dancing belly received a load that made her feel that heaven and earth were in conjunction on the fiery bed of hell. We stripped bare, and I threw the hot bellied girl again on her back and put her lover's prick into her slit. I then knelt with my gaping grotto over her face, and with her late gizzard tickler plunged into it, I felt her licking my well-filled cunt and my stallion's flying shaft, till as he was spending I jerked it out and stuck it in her face, watching her with one black giant in her cunt and a sperming spigot in her eager mouth.

One of the blacks threw himself on the girl, pierced her with his rampant prick, then rolled over on the ground, finally stopped with Mary on top, till, with a lustful cry she sprang up and squatted over his mouth, and seized his fallen monarch reeking with albumen in her mouth.

The other darky picked me up and, belly to belly started running, forcing his prick in me as we went, and fucked me on the fly until we spent. Then he dropped me on my elbows, seized my legs and spiked as I was turned completely over and continued to fuck me till, exhausted, he fell beside me and licked my lust laden slit as I sucked his giant prick.

Enough! Dear Captain Jack! If this works on you as it does on me, all the squaws on the plains will be giving birth to Little Jack Gardners, Jr.

Still with the bunch; when your next furlough comes we will welcome you.

I will not justify myself for writing frankly, for my voluptuous soul snaps its fingers in the face of respectability.

I am made of flesh and blood, and all it can accomplish, on pleasure bent, I would experience.

Pucker, poor prude! Pinch yourself in the dark, under the bed clothes, run away from a man in his shirt-sleeves—but for me—give him to me flesh to flesh, lips to lips, breast to breast, belly to belly, and his bold, blissful cock carrying rapture to my ever yearning cunt—I live for lust alone!

Gus Tolman

PART ONE

Gus Tolman had a remarkably sympathetic touch, highly developed through becoming a pianist of acknowledged excellence where touch with him was his compelling force and accomplishment. It was often said that his touch could bring tears or laughter to an audience, especially could he arouse the erotic emotions in women when he played for impressionable types. His touch had that delicate, insinuating, velvety quality that when applied to any sensitive part of an impressionable woman's anatomy, she became intoxicated with his virility. Let us visualize the physical Tolman.

He was of commanding physique, with a face not exactly handsome, but strikingly attractive due to his personality and virile magnetism. He held every woman spellbound. Added to these attributes, Gus had remarkably developed sexual equipment, over which he experienced and exercised an unusual control. He possessed from youth an unusual and very abnormal penis and a pair of testicles, which of course developed as he used them. When in a state of erection his penis was fully eight inches long and two inches thick and its appendages solid and lightly hung in a most attractively wrinkled skin; all being decorated with brown silky curls. As one woman born in this world of experience once said, she never had felt nor seen such a fascinating and virile sexual equipment so highly developed—that no normal woman who once saw it or felt its velvety flesh and abnormal power could resist it.

To most women, one man's sexual affair was about the same as any other, but with this man it was entirely different.

When in a state of placid rest his was just as attractive and fascinating as when erect and ready to perform its pleasurable function; being so because the head was always uncovered and plum-shaped and prettily mottled. It was, in a flaccid condition, about an inch thick and five or six inches long, hanging like a curved snout over his large wrinkled balls. It was never flabby like most men's, but firm and springy with life. The remarkable control which he had over his joy-giver was manifested in the way he could make the head, when excessively turgid and ferocious, shrink to a size where it could be inserted in the small and tight orifice of a woman without injury, then when completely sheathed, make it expand and harden till every crevice of the quivering slit was crammed full.

Another remarkable faculty Gus had was to retain a rigid condition after discharging his delicious spend. This faculty made Gus a veritable paragon with women who were fortunate enough to experience its wonderful effect in his arms, in the long drawn-out feast of fleshy indulgence. With this method Gus could intoxicate his partner with transports of the wildest joy and supreme ecstasy. He has been referred to as a three-hour model of Priapic glory.

He never believed in taking more pleasure in the form of ecstatic thrills than he gave, always mindful of the salacious and lustful side of a woman's nature, once she became a willing participant and allowed her sexual feelings a free hand. A man who can indulge a woman's secret sexual propensity and pent-up passion by prolonging the rapturous, ravishing feast is always looked upon as an Adonis of supreme delight, and this wonderman was as rare in the art of giving sexual pleasure in a full measure as it is rare to find a woman who does not enjoy it to the point of satiation.

Every woman will take and revel in the bestial indulgence such as he could give her. So it is not to be wondered at if Gus accomplished such abnormal stunts as are told in this story of his life.

The temptress who first turned Gus Tolman's head and caused lecherous thoughts to dominate him is pictured in this story.

Plump, where attractive plumpness was intended to be, making tantalizing, inviting dimples form a kissable mouth with soft, sensuous, curving lips, with their expression constantly changing with every gleam of her passionate eyes; all maddening to any young youth who once realized the fleshy thoughts suggested in such a female.

In an hour of reminiscing Gus related the following episode:

* * *

The type of woman who seemed most desirable to me for some time was richly developed and voluptuously formed; one with soft plump charms enhanced by bewitching dimples and alluring white flesh in which appeared cuddly valleys. Not the overripe, fleshy type, but one whose charms suggested voluptuous pleasures, the well-knit, gracefully proportioned, symmetrical figure with lusciously rounded parts pleasing not only to the carnal eye, but as well to the artist, who appreciated the physical, sensuous delights suggested in such a figure. My mind naturally pictured in addition to such a delectable creature, a healthy body with vigor and a full appreciation of sexual matters, having a vivid, passionate nature. Quite naturally a youth of my temperament met the most satisfying female, or, what seemed to me, the most satisfying woman.

I met such a lady when at a boarding school at the age of seventeen and while there I learned a lot about sexual relations and pleasures derived therefrom through older schoolmates, who would relate, after returning from their city homes, their experience with girls. At such times we would gather in one of our rooms and during the vivid descriptions of female loveliness and lurid word pictures of the lustful scenes, invariably every boy would get an erection, so rampant that we would relieve one another with the hand or masturbate ourselves, getting lascivious excitement and pleasure in watching each other shoot his charge of youthful sap in hissing jets. One boy of nineteen, a handsome chap, inclined to be somewhat of a sissy, admired my sexual organ and displayed a desire to handle it and caress me. On one occasion, during a recital of one of those evenings of lewd pleasures, he persuaded me to sleep with him. I didn't suspect or know why until we were stripped for bed, and he, Harry by name, related his experience with married women and girls, who preferred a skillful tongue to a man's penis. We got so horny and rampant that he took my turgid prick in his mouth and by skillful tonguing, brought on an orgasm and sucked out the last drops of a hot scorching spend. Such indulgences of youthful passion might have fixed in me a taste and habit for such unnatural gratification, had it not been for the intervention of the attractive, seductive, buxom female already mentioned. She was thirty-six and lived in the village where the boarding school was located. This rural beauty was a fair specimen of the type that dominated me pretty much throughout my life. To me she became a standard of female loveliness by which I judged all others, with variations on the one attractive feature, namely, sensuous flesh and softly rounded charms that always seduce men. I used to spend evenings at her home, an old-fashioned house with a big veranda on which hung a hammock couch.

One warm evening in April I was sitting on the edge of the veranda, very near this couch in which Carrie Sexton was sitting, lazily and seductively swinging her feet. It was on this particular occasion that she created in me a fixed appetite for natural gratification of the lustful desires and answered "the call of the flesh." She implanted in my impressionable nature a keen appreciation of the robust, voluptuous type of female, always neatly and attractively attired and scrupulously clean and appetizing, which was always to me one of the most essential qualities to make a girl or woman desirable and thoroughly enjoyable.

That particular evening Carrie wore a dark dress of clinging material which set off her figure alluringly. The waist was cut low in the back and front, with short, loose sleeves which left her plump white arms bare almost to the shoulders, revealing pretty, dimpled elbows. She wore low patent leather slippers and white stockings of silk with openwork at the ankles and feet. I shall never forget her handsomely shaped legs, so prettily rounded in those gauzy diaphanous silk stockings, through which the ravishing pink-white of her lovely skin sifted so alluringly. I thought Carrie was the most ravishing vision of female loveliness I would ever meet. From where I sat, I commanded a most inflaming view of those beautiful, shapely legs.

Right here let me dwell on the subject of legs. To me, at most times, a girl's or woman's legs, if she attracted me at all, played a prominent part in the quest of the illusive charm nestled between them. Slender legs seldom attracted me unless they were seductively pretty with trim, graceful ankles and swelling calves. To me a lean, skinny figure was always like a chicken bone with no meat on it; a disappointment to a man whose appetite for sensuous, plump charms demanded a gratifying repast. There is always a scant satisfaction between slender, shapely legs, unless the owner of them has abnormal skill in the sexual act. Ah! give me the sumptuously formed female with strong, shapely legs who knows how to cuddle and produce those voluptuous thrills with well defined appreciation of her sensuous charms in which I can wallow with ravishing delight. Then, too, how enticing are the dimples in fat knees. One rarely sees dimples in skinny knees. Then too, the way in which a girl or woman uses her legs is an added attraction. The demure damsel rarely thinks of her legs. They rarely have little to say beyond what they recall as flesh and bone; but a young woman who is conscious of having attractive legs will always use them to the best advantage by displaying their good qualities. She knows how to flirt with her legs, once she observes that a man is looking at them. Many a conquest has been made by pretty young women by seducing a man with their sensitively enticing legs.

The question is often heard, "Why is a man always eager to look at a woman's legs?" I have often, myself, wondered. Here is my answer. Legs have a language. They speak volumes. They are the speaking charms that are so ingratiating in the supreme enjoyment of the sexual act. If pretty, they usually suggest a sensuous wealth of charms above the knee and entice a man to conjure in his mind the delights of feeling and caressing the charms of the sensuously plump, shapely leg. The thought of fondling or gazing on a well formed leg causes an irresistible desire to possess it. And after all, a sexual, lustful sensation is what every man loves and craves. One hates to imagine and cannot conjure up any great enthusiasm over slim, unshapely legs. There is no warmth or sympathy suggested.

It was that wonderful thrill I experienced when I first became intimately aware of the language of the legs that made me ever on the alert to see a pretty leg. Carrie Sexton's legs engaged my carnal thoughts that were rapidly developing. They infatuated me, enthralled me that evening on the veranda. Those fascinating legs drew me like a magnet. I immediately longed to feel them. They were within reach. I felt my eyes smart with increasing emotion as I gloated. My hands fairly tingled with desire to mold the perfectly rounded, plump calf and enjoy the feeling of the voluptuously filled hosiery.

It was all so new to me, I was bashful, but in a moment of boldness I reached over and clasped Carrie's trim ankle in my hand. I got bolder and slipped my hand up and around the plump soft calf. I felt a thrill go straight through me to my impressionable young penis.

The buxom woman never stirred. Carrie was an abnormally amorous girl. She evidently enjoyed my boyish desires and the impetuous liberties I took. She was obviously aware that her legs were exercising an influence over me, and in fact, those wonderfully handsome legs were actually crying out to be fondled. They seemed to say, "feel me, feel me all the way up."

I perceived a shudder run down the leg I was squeezing. She gasped. I heard the soft words, "Oh, Gus." I imagined that she objected. I was at once afraid that she would repulse me and I withdrew my hand. She stealthily drew her dress up till I saw her knees and a glimpse of the white flesh bare above her stockings. It acted like a subtle picture of my willpower and overcame my bashfulness and fear. Carrie saw the effect on me in my leering eyes. She spoke in a trembling and subdued voice. Her eyes were filled with a lurid light. I know now that it was "the call of the flesh" shining from eyes aglow with lustful emotions.

"Tell me, Gussie, do you like to look at my legs? Do you like them?"

"Oh, Miss Carrie," I replied, "I think that they are lovely, and they are so delicious to feel."

"Then Gussie, you may fondle them again,

I like to feel your hand. Do it again." My fears passed, and I got bolder and moved closer to give me greater ease and freer use of my hands. Carrie, observing my object in drawing closer, spoke up boldly, moving closer to the end of the couch to make room for me, and said:

"Come Gussie, sit beside me here, then you can enjoy me more comfortably." I responded with boyish delight. Instead of sitting up, the amorous Carrie stretched out in a recumbent position and suggested that I lie beside her, which I did. One of her lovely, plump bare arms was about my neck. Oh, how I trembled with a strange emotion as I felt the cool soft flesh of that soft arm and the curving contours of her twisting sensuous body as it settled against me.

"Now Gussie," she began, "you can fondle me and love me as much as you like." Of course I wanted to reach her legs. She was quick to read my thoughts. Pulling her dress clear up, she threw one leg over me. My hand touched the full rounded calf. Emboldened, I slipped my hand up over the fat knee. My fingers touched the soft velvety skin above. Then I squeezed the plump firm flesh. I felt a wave of tremulous excitement go through me and center in every fiber of my turgid penis. I trembled with uncontrollable emotion. Carrie knowingly sensed my condition and she too trembled as she seductively spoke, "Oh Gussie, your hand makes me feel lovely. How nice that feels. Oh, don't be bashful Gus, put your hand farther up."

Her ardent reassurance made me forget everything. I slipped my hand farther up along Carrie's smooth robust thighs. It encountered no barriers until it reached the swelling cheek of a fat round buttock. Here, the tight edge of her drawers prevented further progress. Carrie raised her leg and wriggled onto her back saying, "There Gus, fondle my cunnie." It was the first time that I had heard that name given to a girl's sexual organ. My hand trembled as I gingerly sought the unfamiliar and to me, unknown spot in which centered a woman's most impressionable nature.

I felt for the first time in my career, that charm of all charms and magnet which draws all men to its delectable delights, a woman's silky-haired and thickly tufted pussy. Its protruding mound was hard, but just below, my fingers encountered exquisitely soft and pulpy lips into which my fingers instinctively sank. It was most enticing to me. Curious as I always was, I explored. My middle finger easily slipped into a tight and puckering orifice.

It was hot and juicy. I impulsively pressed my turgid aching penis against Carrie's thighs. She felt it and writhed, and in a soft tender voice said: "Oh, Gussie, how lovely your finger feels." Reaching down she placed her hand on the swelling in my trousers. "Oh, Gus," she said with feeling, "what a big hard thing you have. Wouldn't you like to put it where your finger is?"

I answered in a fluttering voice, "Oh, Miss Carrie, I—I'm afraid, I—I never thought of such a thing before."

"Why, Gussie," she asked, "how do you boys take the stiffness out of your things when they get hard?"

I boldly replied, "We jerk off."

"Oh, Gussie, that is all wrong," she gasped. "and naughty and unnecessary when you can get a nice girl to do it with her thing."

"How?" I asked.

"Come over on top of me and I'll show you," she answered. It was too dark to see her face plainly, but I could still see those big blue eyes and ruddy lips of Carrie's as she proceeded to unfasten my pants and take out my highly inflamed penis. For my age I had a large one, and knew by actual measurement it was nearly five inches long when stiff and about an inch thick. I was known in school as "heavy hung Gus." Carrie gave a smothered scream and exclaimed, "Heavens, Gus, it's beautiful, it's so big. Come on and get on top and put it into me." Carrie was strong and lusty. She almost lifted me up, and opening her lovely thighs I fell between them. She hugged me and drew my face to hers. "Kiss me, Gussie," she whispered. It was my first kiss of passion. Her lips parted slightly. Oh, God! I shall never forget that kiss. With moist and mellow lips she almost sucked my breath away. Her velvet tongue darted in and out. I never knew how it happened, but instinctively my painfully stiff penis glided into the juicy lips of Carrie's hungry pussy. It is impossible to describe the sensations that swept over me. I thought I wanted to pee. I got frightened and breathlessly murmured, "Oh—Oh, Miss Carrie, I'm going to pee. Let me out."

She replied by holding me tighter with her sturdy legs. "It ain't pee, Gussie, it's your sweet lovely juice," she whispered as she worked her pussy up and down. "Move it in and out, dear, it's lovely—Oh—Oh—do it fast."

Her big bosoms heaved; she panted and kissed and moaned as I instinctively proceeded to perform the sexual act. My tool glided in and out most lusciously until I was bewildered with ecstatic thrills. I remember how well Carrie was affected—how she panted and tightened her robust legs and arms about me. I felt her hot breath on my face—her soft lips quivered and her tongue filled my mouth and, right before I experienced my first natural orgasm, Carrie, overwhelmed with the delights of frictional activity, gave little soft screams and a long sigh as she died away in a blissful spend. Although young and inexperienced, I was impressed, especially when her convulsed pussy shut tight on my penis and I couldn't move. Oh, how queer I felt. In a minute or two Carrie seemed to recover and softly spoke, "Gus, that was lovely. Do it again, you haven't come yet. Oh, do it fast."

Her tight hole relaxed, and I moved my bottom up and down. I thrust with rapid strokes. I could feel my hair curl and my scalp wrinkle. My toes worked. I clutched her in my arms. I moaned and gasped, for that wonderful first spend in a woman was at hand. I couldn't see. All was dark. Then every part of me seemed to explode and a rush of sap seemed to rush from my brain centers and heart and burst in my painful balls.

Oh, God! How entrancing it was as the hot juice gushed through and out of my bursting penis. I couldn't speak. I heard Carrie squeal, as her pussy opened and closed in spasms. Her womb was pressed to the point of my penis. She gasped and shuddered. "Oh—oo—oo! Oh, God! —how—lovely—I—I—come—oo—Oh!"

All was still. I lay on the panting voluptuous form of Carrie in a swoon. Those little nips and twitches of her limbs and pinching hole made me see stars and dizzy as they sucked the remaining drops of my first natural spend. After I recovered I concluded that there was no gratification of passion like the one secured between a woman's legs.

From then on I became a slave to the female sex, and a wild devotee of the charms of legs and the fluffy little plaything between them. Carrie and I spent many a happy and fruitful afternoon on strolls in the woods on a mountain, back of the village.

She kept my lustful desire at fever heat by showing her beautiful legs and displaying the sensuous curves of her buxom form on every slight pretext. She was one of the most amorous and salacious women I ever knew. Gee! How she did love a stiff penis. I shall never forget how she created in me an appreciation of the charm of a woman's breasts and what they afforded me in the pursuit of lustful pleasures. For a long time, however, the female bust did not attract me for my mind was always centered on legs. In lascivious dreams I always saw legs, but later on, a buxom pair of bubbies were added to my fanciful dreams. Carrie never went with me to the woods that she didn't seduce me into gratifying her passions and mine. There was always a piquant flavor to a diddle on the grass. On one occasion when I was exploring the charms of Carrie's handsome legs during one of our strolls in the woods, I expressed a wish to see her naked. Of course it was too risky to attempt such a thing when she might be observed by others, but Carrie's amorous and lewd mind was inflamed and she quickly replied:

"Well, Gussie, you are getting to be a man and ought to see a girl's form. How'd you like to see my breasts and fondle them?"

"Oh," I gasped, "does a man like a woman's breasts?"

"I'll show you, Gus, then you'll know," she replied.

We soon came to a cave where we could indulge in wanton and lustful pleasures in safety. Carrie sat on a boulder and quite innocently removed her waist, then her corset and lastly her chemise. I shall never forget the alabaster flesh and delicate blue veins of her beautifully rounded shoulders and arms. My eyes were fastened with wonder and lascivious amazement on the snowy bosoms of that voluptuous young wanton. I gloated. The bright red buttons, her nipples, looked like strawberries. They fascinated me. The moment I touched the plump, firm, round forms and those stiff nipples between my fingers as I molded the alabaster velvety globes, I felt a thrill clear to my toes and my impressionable prick stiffened and got as hard as iron.

My youthful desires were inflamed to a high pitch as I got bolder and fondled Carrie's barren charms.

"Oh, Gussie," she exclaimed. "You make my pussy itch." Catching sight of the swelling in my pants, she blushed and pantingly exclaimed: "Gus, your pretty prick is so lovely and big, put it between my bubbies." She unbuttoned my pants forthwith, and with trembling fingers she drew it out and kissed it. I stood in front of her straddling her thighs. I placed my turgid tool between her milky bubbies, and Carrie, with a lewd leer, pressed the pulpy globes around it. As I gloated on the lustful picture, Carrie tickled my tight hard balls. She evidently wanted to make me spend between her big bubbies. I wanted to, but a natural aversion to spilling my sap all over her neck and bosom made me hold back. It was then that I found that I could restrain the impulse to spend and prolong the sensations of erotic pleasure, wishing to have the ecstatic thrills of a complete orgasm in the proper place. The longer I held back the more passionate Carrie became. "Oh, Gus," she cried out, "get on top of me and do it." She laid down on a thick bed of leaves, pulled her skirts above her waist and spread her lovely thighs apart.

I then saw for the first time the marvelous enticing spot that a man risks all to possess. Carrie was naked to the waist. My lusty prick was throbbing and swollen to the bursting point. "Come, Gussie," she said, and I fell on her and buried my burning tool to the hilt. With one hand on a lovely soft bubbie and my mouth glued to hers, I fucked like a mad bull. Ye Gods, how she heaved and groaned. I was like a ferocious animal.

The seclusion of the place allowed wild and lustful expressions. Carrie screamed and bit my face and neck in her frenzy. She spent twice, long before I was ready to let it come, and when I did I was blind and drunk with lewd delight. My God, how I did go off and shoot the rich sperm into her belly. I came to after a delicious die-away, in which I enjoyed most sensuously her bared charms and clinging legs. When I got up I was so faint I almost tottered. Carrie wiped my tool and dried her curly juice-covered slit with her handkerchief. That feast of flesh in the cave will linger forever in my memory.

One evening while sitting on Carrie's veranda and feasting my eyes on her pretty ankles and artfully exposed calf, as well as the sensuous curves and contours of her form, a young and very pretty girl passed. I was attracted by her legs. They were large and exquisitely shaped and perfectly molded in blue silk hosiery. Being quite young, her dress was short, exposing a pair of nice fat knees. The swing and twitch of her skirt revealed momentarily glimpses of the bare white skin of her upper thighs. I noticed that the girl had large, plump bubbies and she wore very short sleeves showing her pretty plump arms. Carrie saw me gloating. "Say, Gussie," she laughingly said, "that's little Grace Merrill. Hasn't she got nice legs?"

"Dandy," I said, "I'd like to feel them and squeeze those nice breasts of hers."

"Alright, Gus. I'll call her over." Grace came and sat in a rocking chair near me. She was some relation of Carrie's who apparently knew that Grace was not averse to amorous dalliance with boys.

"Say, Grace," Carrie said, "Gus thinks that you have very pretty legs and titties. He wants to feel of them."

Grace blushed and kicked her pretty legs in the air in a coquettish manner. Sitting where I did, I saw clear up under her clothes and the white plump flesh of her delicious thighs. It made me wild. My prick was getting stiff and hard as a bar of iron, and it showed provokingly.

I got bold and put my hand on her shapely calf and slid it up and down.

"Oh, Gus," she giggled, "you tickle me." Up went my hand to the bare flesh. It was like a baby's. I pinched and Grace squirmed.

"Oh, Aunt Carrie," exclaimed the unsophisticated girl, "he's making me feel funny."

"Yes, Grace, and look at the front of his pants. You are making his thing get big and stiff." Now, all country girls are pretty well acquainted with sexual matters through contact with nature, which is never concealed on the farms, and though Grace knew what a boy's thing was for and she knew also what her little thing was for, so when her eyes rested on the bulging place between my legs, her eyes got big. She gazed long at it and then said:

"Oh, Aunt Carrie, he's got an awful big one; how I'd like to see it."

"Come up here, Gussie," said Carrie, "and sit in the hammock and let Grace see your lovely peg." You can bet I was not bashful, but quickly complied, and Grace's eyes were riveted in amazement on my tool, which was far larger than she had ever seen or dreamed of amongst the boys in the village.

"Oh—Oh," she exclaimed, giggling, "it's awful. Can I feel of it?"

"Of course," said I, "but you must let me feel yours, too."

Grace was standing by my side. I passed my hand under her petticoat and slipped it up and down her soft smooth thighs to her plump little bottom. It was covered with her drawers and I knew that I couldn't reach it or what I was after. Grace laughed and whispered, "Unbutton my drawers, Gussie, then you can feel my thing."

As I did so, Grace clasped her chubby fingers around my penis and gasped and trembled. Gosh, how delicious her hand felt to my hot and turgid penis. The first touch and squeeze almost made me go off, but my mind was centered on getting at the girlish slit between those fascinating legs.

She was handling and testing the stiffness of my prick when my searching fingers crept between the soft cheeks of her bottom and found the girl's young slit. It was fat and had hard, thick lips like rubber, but there was no long hair on it, just a little soft down. Oh, my, what a cute and seductive little cunnie she had. I got a finger in between the elastic lips and found a tiny hole. Grace trembled, and writhed and giggled. "Oh, Aunt Carrie, he's doing it with his finger."

I was working my finger in and out. Carrie spoke: "That's right. Let him do it and it will make you feel good. If you want to see Gussie's sap come, just move your hand up and down his thing and jerk him off." Ye Gods, that charming girl masturbated me like a expert. I felt ashamed to let a girl see me spend, but my lustful appetite got the better of me and I just let Grace amuse herself. Carrie was unfastening Grace's waist to release her firm young bubbies that were standing out like rocks. When I saw them pop out my first impulse was to feel and bite the snowy red-tipped globes, which I did and I got one stiff little nipple in my mouth. Grace was minutely examining my prick and balls which she rolled about in her fingers, till I was frantic for that friction which brings on the delightful thrill of a spend. In my impetuous lust I cried out: "Jerk me off, Grace, don't make me wait. Jerk it and see the juice come." That was what we boys always called the semen.

Grace was restless, her big blue eyes and cherry lips began to get a dreamy trembling expression for my middle finger was being thrust in and out of her tight little cunnie. She held my prick stiff and tight in her hand and began to jerk. As her feelings became more and more intense her hand moved up and down more rapidly. It was a tense and lurid moment. I felt her fat bottom pinch and quiver. Her legs shook. She laughed and gasped and cried out: "Oh, Gus—sie—Aunt—Car—rie—I—I—I'm—I—I." Just then the climax came to my highly inflamed emotions. I groaned, my balls smarted, then a rush of semen came and squirted in pearly hissing jets. Grace almost swooned when she saw it, and I felt a warm, soft gush of her girlish juice wet my finger. Carrie caught her as she was about to fall in a faint. I didn't linger there, but hastened back to my room and to bed to dream of legs, bubbies and young girls' quivering cunnies.

The next time I saw Carrie, she said that Grace was terribly in love with me and wanted to have some more pleasure. I remembered asking Carrie if Grace would let me do it to her, to which she replied:

"Of course she will, but you must be careful, she is only fifteen and she may be a virgin." My next thought was to induce Grace to go with me to that cave on the mountain. I had no difficulty, but she seemed so in love and amorous that she agreed to any plan to be alone with me. I arranged to have her meet me on the edge of the woods on a Saturday afternoon when all the boys would be sure to be in the village and no one would, by any chance, be in that cave. When I met Grace she looked lovely. She wore a Tam o' Shanter hat, a tight fitting sweater-jacket, a short flannel dress, and her plump shapely legs were in tempting red silk stockings.

Imagine a pretty young girl so attired, with

a pair of strong hard bubbies standing out round and stiff under her jacket and a pair of stunningly pretty legs. And the same girl, panting and quivering with jubilant, hot youth, crying out for the gratification of its "call of the flesh," and being answered by an impressionable young man of nineteen tingling with animal passion. You can imagine how I felt, knowing this amorous love-sick maiden desired me.

When we came to the cave we rushed into each other's arms. Her soft sensuous young body was molded to me as our lips met in a long hot kiss.

"Oh, Gussie," she gurgled, trembling all over. "Will you love me always?"

"Yes, Grace," I replied, "forever, and be your sweetheart. Will you do everything?"

"Oh, yes—yes, Gus!" she fluttered, "everything. I love you so I'll do everything you wish."

In my eagerness I ruthlessly tore off her jacket. Ye Gods, there was nothing under it. Her lovely body was bare to the waist. I almost devoured her luscious bubbies and velvety shoulders with kisses. I fondled those peachy charms and spreading the jacket on the thick piles of leaves where I had enjoyed Carrie, I begged Grace to lay down. As she did so I pushed her clothes up, unbuttoned her drawers and removed them. I shall never forget the delicious prick-teasing picture spread out under my eyes, burning with youthful lust. No doubt came to me of the right to take what was offered. I didn't know what being a virgin meant. The seductive banquet of girlish charms offered in that moment and in that position maddened me. I gloated, fascinated with the lovely whiteness and plumpness of those bare thighs and especially did I gaze with lustful emotion on the girl's sexual charm. How seductive it was and how cute the deep slit cut in the plump flesh looked surrounded by a slight thin growth of down. That maddening slit in the pulpy lips extending below hid itself between the fat cheeks of the girl's plump little bottom. Something filled me with a passionate desire to kiss the dimpled white round belly and cute deep slit. I fell on my knees, and fondled her legs and belly. "Ah, Grace, it's so pretty, I want to kiss it."

"Oh, Gussie," she spoke softly, "kiss it if you wish, I love you so." It was a wonderful introduction to my growing appreciation and lust for flesh. I passionately kissed her dimpled belly, then my mouth passed on downward over Grace's prominent mound. It was hard. When my lips touched those of her cunning little pussy I shivered. I always thought it might be repugnant to kiss a girl between the legs, but Grace was so pretty, and sweet and clean there I just loved it and the odor I detected was fascinating to me.

I shall never know what made me do it, but I thrust my tongue in that tiny hole and worked it all about. Grace was trembling and moaning. The longer I held my tongue to her, the longer I wanted to. It must have so inflamed and titillated Grace that an orgasm was produced, for she wound her legs about me, shivered, and cried out: "Oh, darling—Oh—how lovely—oo—Oh!" and then she relaxed.

A warm little gush of her girlish juices gathered on my tongue. It made me frantic. My pego was in agony, and my balls smarted. I jumped on top of the half-fainting girl and taking my tool in one hand, guided it to the pouting orifice and ferociously shoved it in. Ye Gods! How I went off as I struggled to bury my prick to its very root. Grace gave a shriek, clasped me in her arms and cried out in agony: "Oh, Gus, take it out. It's killing me. Oh—Oh, don't do it any more!"

Her spend mingled with mine, lubricated the way and once buried, my tool was pinched and snuggled most delightfully. I lay still for a while with my first frenzied spend but my tool lost none of its stiffness. I was a youth with unbridled, vigorous passion and right then I studied and used my abnormal powers.

Gradually Grace's pain subsided, her cries became soft sweet moans and she kissed me ardently, then in a fluttering voice spoke these caressing words, which I shall never forget: "Oh, darling Gus, isn't it lovely? I love you so I could have died. Oh, Gussie, do it fast!"

I didn't move. I was too blissfully contented, but the itch for friction put fire in my whole body. Grace craved the pleasurable friction in her tight little cunnie and, either by instinct or intuition she began to work her belly and hips up and down. It was then that I realized how lovely it was to feel a bare belly rubbing against mine, and the nipping jerks of a hot cunt. Heavens how she wriggled and heaved, how I devoured that girl's lips and mauled her fine bubbies. My brain reeled. I didn't move, I was so entranced. That friction so applied, quickly brought our youthful passion to a climax. I remembered our cries of ecstasy and agonizing groans of delirious sensuous joy mingled as we both came together. Ye Gods, how lusciously and thrillingly my semen poured into Grace.

How sweetly she responded with quivering limbs and twitching belly. How her eyes rolled just as everything got dark and we seemed to fuse into one body. I remember how I exclaimed in my implusive emotion—"Oh, Grace, I love you—I love you," and her lips managed to quiver out her reply, "I love you, too, Gussie, I'm your little wife now." She smiled through her tears of joy.

When I withdrew and stood up, I discovered what a havoc I had done, for her gratified passionate pussy was covered with blood and so was my limp penis. I was frightened and began to cry—"Oh, don't cry, Gussie—it's only blood from my maidenhead—every girl has to lose it, and I love you and was happy to let you have it, so don't cry."

I then and there resolved to never seduce a virgin. I procured water from a spring nearby and with my handkerchief I wiped away all traces of blood and I keep the cloth to this day as a memento of my first real love-fuck.

Of all my adventures and feasting of flesh I never had such an exquisite and ravishing girl in my life. No full grown woman can put into her movements the exquisite flavor and soul-stirring snap a young girl can in her first flush of love—the impetuous wriggle of her untrained and twisting back produced sensations no boy ever forgets, especially when the frenzied nips and strong impulsive suction of her loving little cunnie extracts the delirious sap from his very soul. I enjoyed Grace many times after that and she became most lustfully proficient in her sexual pleasures.

Carrie taught me many artful and skillful tricks in the indulgence of the flesh, but when

I discovered she was being fucked by two other fellows in the town, my fondness for her ceased.

At the end of the school term I went with my parents to the mountains for the summer, where I had many chances to indulge my rapidly developing passion for female charms.

Mary, our family cook, went with us to our summer home. Up to this time Mary had never shown any interest in me, but as I had had some experience in sexual pleasures and my appreciation for female charms had developed appreciably, the charms of Mary came under my vision with their full meaning and effect. I lost no opportunity to gloat on her for she had a form that would attract any man. She was Irish and mighty good looking. Though a cook, she had the makeup of an exceptional type of servant and acted in the Tolman family as governess as well as cook, so that she was in my company quite frequently. When I observed what a handsomely shaped leg she had I sought every opportunity to be with her. The first occasion was when Mary and I went for a walk to the river. We had to climb several fences, and Mary, not thinking, made a good effort to climb over. I was just behind her. When she threw her leg over, her skirts drew up, and the other leg was exposed nearly to her hip.

She had on brown silk stockings, gartered below the knee and short lacy white drawers, which clung snugly to the robust thighs. Her bare knees were fat and most ravishingly pink. She had an ankle and calf that for perfection in contour and shape were matchless. When she finally got over, her skirts caught on the top rail, and I now saw in all its splendor her magnificent bottom sticking out through the opening of her tightly stretched drawers. The deep valley between the round, fat and dimpled cheeks like snowy globes made me gloat in amazement, and my unruly penis got hard as iron. My first thought was a piece of that glowing, ravishing part of her anatomy, and I felt impelled to feel of it.

Mary had screamed in her predicament and then called to me for help. Instead of helping her first, I passed my hand over the smooth polished surface of her bottom, and then dug my fingers in under and between her plump thighs. Again she screamed and remonstrated. "Gussie, stop, you are bad and naughty. Stop it!"

"Oh, no," I said, "I'm going to feel it, you are so lovely, that I am going to feel your thing. Ah, what a fine one you'd make—May I Mary? Let me do it?"

Mary was now laughing and tugging at her skirts. "If you don't stop and loosen my skirts, Gus, I'll tell your mother. You ought to be thrashed good," said Mary, blushing.

I pinched the soft, firm flesh, and again dug my fingers into the pulpy, juicy lips of her pouting cunnie. Mary's buxom bottom was crimson and twisting as she laughed and choked down her rapidly increasing emotions. No sexually vigorous woman could easily resist the magnetic touches of a man. Her resistance and remonstrance became less and less as I continued to poke and manipulate the susceptible Mary, who was by nature, amorous and passionate once she was aroused.

"Oh, Gus, you are so bad. Let me down and I'll let you feel me more." I thought this was a ruse to get me to cease so I continued. I know my eyes were aflame and my prick was almost bursting. With my free hand I grabbed Mary's big bubbies through a waist that was very thin. My fingers were working rapidly in the juicy depths when I heard her moan and then softly murmur: "Oh, Gussie—I—I—I'm—Oh—oo." I then felt a gush of spend on my fingers, after which I released her skirts. She turned to face me. Her face was aflame from the effects of a premature, unsatisfied orgasm.

"Gussie, you are so bad, I shall either whip you or tell your mother."

"No, no, Mary," I exclaimed, for I was rabid by now. "Whip me if you wish." Her face was aglow with erotic emotion and assumed anger. Seeing some bushes, Mary easily broke a whip off and clutching me by the arm, she led me to a stump in the woods on which she sat down and directed me to lower my pants and lie across her knees. I was a full grown lad and, of course, did not feel that that licking was due me, but my passion, and the itch for adventure quickly led me to do anything that would satisfy my lustful nature and appetites. Mary had pulled her dress clear up above her knees, presumably to punish and tantalize me, by showing as much of her legs as possible. I lowered my trousers and when Mary caught sight of my manly rod, rampantly bounding and rearing its ruby head, she gasped and laughed with a tremble in her voice, as she exclaimed: "Gus, how dare you show that awful thing to me? Come here. Lie over my knees. I'll show you how to behave yourself next time."

I did as I was told, and presented my bottom for Mary to whip, at the same time running my hands up and down Mary's attractive legs. She was trembling as she began to tantalize and chastise me with light blows of the whip. "Ouch! Wow!" I yelled. "Gee, Mary, why be so cruel, when we could be having some fun now. Ouch."

"There Gus, take that and that," she said, as she whacked away with the whip. "Will you behave now? Does it hurt you?"

"No not there," I howled. "It hurts in my prick. Gosh, you are mean when a fellow wants a piece."

"Say, Gussie, I never heard you talk like that before. Why, its awful. Stop pinching my legs!" Whack, swish, whack came the rod on my bottom. Mary felt the hot knob against her leg. Reaching down her left hand she clasped her fingers about it. "Oh golly, Mary," I said, "jerk me off. I could screw a knot hole, I'm so hot." Mary dropped the whip and reached down between my legs and rolled my hard balls in her fingers and gently manipulated my penis till I was relieved and shot a wild delirious shot of semen all over her hand and thigh. I groaned under the force of a severe orgasm.

"Oh, Gus, you nasty thing. You've squirted a lot of sticky stuff all over me. Oh, Gus—sie—mine is com—coming, too—Ah—there—there—it—comes!"

The lewd and sensuous scene had so inflamed her mind and passion that she, too, had experienced an orgasm.

"There Gus get up. You and I have been dreadfully naughty and you must never let me see your awful thing again." Mary returned to the house at once and I followed later. My bottom smarted so that evening, that my penis was constantly stiff. Mary's room was next to mine and as everyone in the house had gone to bed, in my highly inflamed condition I felt tempted to steal into Mary's room.

I was undressed and ready for bed when I heard Mary pouring water for a sponge bath. At once the thought came to me that she would be undressed, so quietly stealing forth, I tried her door and found it unlocked. Bold and daringly, led on by erotic emotions, I entered stealthily. Mary was standing stark naked before her wash stand and before she knew it I had my arms around her. My nightgown was open and my rampant penis jabbed her velvety rump.

Mary gave a smothered scream: "Stop it, Gussie. Stop this foolish business and go to bed. Stop it I say!" she said angrily.

"No, I shan't," I replied, "it's all your fault. You made me so passionately hot today with that whipping, I can't go to bed. I want to fuck you." And then my hand slipped down over Mary's smooth belly to that tuft that stood out on a full hard mound. The moment my fingers found their way between the soft juicy lips I discovered her prominent clitoris, which felt to me like a little stiff penis. I began to rub it. The sensation produced in Mary was an instantaneous lustful desire. "Wait, Gussie," she whispered, "Let me finish washing and then we'll get into bed."

"Promise me, Mary," I said to her.

"I promise, Gus," replied Mary, trembling all over. I stepped back and removed my nightgown and gloated on my first vision of a woman entirely nude. No youth could have had a more perfect specimen of female wealth of charms on which to gaze and form standards. Mary's body was like alabaster and every line and curve was sensuously lovely. Her beautiful large breasts were firm and springy and tipped with large red stiff nipples that stood out like strawberries. The contour and roundness of her hips, thighs and limbs fascinated me and filled me with lustful thoughts. Especially did my gaze rest on Mary's round white bottom and the tempting, tufted lips of her pussy, showing under and between the large cheeks and robust limbs.

Her glorious bosoms trembled and bounced as she dried herself. I was passionate and my penis was standing straight out with the whole inflamed knob showing in all its turgid condition. When Mary saw it, she uttered a little sigh and said in a low voice: "Gussie, you are an awful bad boy. That lovely big thing would kill a small girl. Come. We will get in bed." I was willing and eager. When she flung herself on the bed, I bounced on her like an eager animal.

"Go slow, Gussie. I'll put it in for you and don't make any noise," she whispered, as she opened her thighs and guided my rigid, straining penis to its proper place, which was juicy and elastic and she soon had it completely sheathed. In my impetuous longing for friction, I began to move my hips up and down to work the aching stiffness in and out. The faster I worked, the more excited we both became. Mary hugged me to her and wound her beautiful legs around me, crushing me close to her in a vise-like grip. I was, like all impetuous youths, too absorbed in the one supreme thought of gratifying my passions to enjoy the full meaning and accompanying delights of a voluptuous woman. I had not yet learned how to indulge in the ravishing banquet of sexual feasting, but Mary had. She panted and, almost breathless, admonished me, "Oh, Gus—sie, don't be in such a hurry or you'll spoil a good fuck." This only tended to make me more furious, but with her clinging arms and legs trembling with amorous, lustful deliberation, held me down to short deep digs in her passionate pussy.

Mary, in her fear of an interrupted, long, drawn out enjoyment, gave way to the delightful digs of impetuous youth and let herself go. Panting and heaving and straining me to her with crushing force, her enforced orgasm came. She whispered in choking exclamations: "Oh, Gus—sie—that's—so—go—go-good—I'm—com—ing—" and then in little gurgling cries, "There—there!"

Everything got black to me, my brain reeled, a delirium submerged me. Mary's cunnie contracted in spasms of blissful spending and sucked my impressionable shaft in her throbbing depths. I let out a cry: "Oh, Gee, Mary, I'm—I—I shall—pee."

"Alright, Gussie, let—the pee come—that's fine—Oh, Gussie, that's cream, not pee," gurgled Mary, as she again spent deliciously when feeling the hot juice of youth gush into her quivering slit.

For a long time I lay in Mary's arms during which she told me how much more enjoyable it is to prolong the pleasure and how to get the greatest enjoyment by playing with a woman, and how to make a woman enjoy it. Mary wantonly showed me the place between her legs and made me kiss it, saying a woman liked to be kissed there as it made her hot. We were both soon eager for another piece. This time I followed instructions and restrained myself into a long drawn out feast. Mary was overjoyed and amorous for she obtained two more lovely spends before I went off, after which I left her and went to my own bed.

We found many opportunities to indulge in our lustful pleasures until finally my parents discovered our sexual relations, and they discharged Mary.

The following year, while at my folks' summer home, I met a stunning brunette, Anna Burton. She was our family doctor's daughter; plump, amorous, and pretty. She had the complexion of a Spaniard; dark and rich in coloring, with a form that made my mouth water and my eyes burn every time that I got a glimpse of her beautiful legs. They were large and exquisitely shaped and her breasts denoted voluptuous bubbies, all of which made my hands tingle with lustful longing to feel and fondle them.

Anna was just tall enough to be in perfect proportion to her build. She had wavy, jet-black hair and a pair of black eyes that shone with a lurid fire of passion, which displayed itself in the swaying undulations of her sensuous body.

She usually wore a short skirt to facilitate her mountain climbing; sturdy tan shoes and tan silk stockings molded her beautiful round shaped legs perfectly without a wrinkle. Anna was about twenty-three and full of ardent spirits, gay and reckless to the point of wanton abandon. She was a most lovable and sympathetic creature and when she met me, she seemed to sense my ardent and lustful nature.

Her sympathies led her into wanton indiscretions, which to her were innocent, but once her warm nature was aroused she became the embodiment of intense sexual passion. Being a doctor's daughter, she had gleaned from his books about all there was to know on sexual matters and what she didn't learn her fertile passionate mind supplied in lurid dreams and visions of sexual pleasures. She had a keen and deep appreciation of what the opposite sex desired, liked and enjoyed. Anna soon observed my nature during our strolls in the woods and mountain climbing, when I would ogle her and gloat on her reckless and wanton exposures. She, of course, knew that she had legs and other charms that were very attractive to men and she was never chary about showing them to advantage, especially her beautiful legs, well defined, exquisitely shaped hips, and bottom. When she discovered that I got a thrill every time she showed more than the occasion required, she would wantonly bring into prominence her lovely contours and manage to expose her plump knees and enough bare flesh above her stockings to make any ordinary man tingle with desire.

The mere fact that she knew that I was watching and took every opportunity to see all that I could, made her feel itchy all over to be caressed and possessed. She understood the expression in the eyes and face of a man when he was inflamed with passion, and I was no exception. My eyes conveyed my feelings and desires in a steady languorous gaze that I fixed on Anna's sensuous and lusciously proportioned contours.

Anna's mouth was molded for sensuous kisses. Her lips were rather full and lusciously red, the even white teeth gleamed when smiles brought laughing dimples to her pretty cheeks. What man could resist the lure of that kissable mouth? I did not, for I was rapidly becoming a connoisseur in the art of kissing and lipping of an amorous female. Coming to a secluded place in the woods beside a small lake one day, I was overwrought with passion, and I got very bold. Anna and I were standing near a large boulder, a flat top rock, absorbed in a playful teasing argument, when Anna smiled, tipped back her head and shot a tormenting inviting flash, full of seductiveness, from her black sparkling eyes. With a sudden impulsive move I had the alluring creature in my arms. Bending her back on the rock I smothered her with passionate kisses. At the same time I molded a firm round bubbie in my hand. Anna gasped and trembled with an emotion that my kisses and touches sent rioting through her hot-blooded form. When I finally got back my breath, I protested a wealth of love for her. "Anna, you sweet lovely thing." She returned my lustful gaze with limpid, half-closed eyes turned up towards me and naively replied:

"Oh, Gus—I love you, too, but I must not let you make love to me." She struggled to her feet and in doing so, her short wide skirts worked up above her knees, showing considerable bare flesh. My ever watchful eye did not miss the alluring lustful view of ravishing legs and bare skin. Emboldened by my success so far, I pushed her stocking down far enough to reveal to my lustful gaze the most ravishing, dimpled, pink and white knee that I ever saw. Anna was instantly affected by the contact and subtle magnetic touch, but startled and fearful of what I might do next, she almost seductively remonstrated: "Why, Gus, aren't you ashamed?"

"No, indeed," I replied. "You've got such handsome legs and such pretty knees, I want to feel them and kiss them. By Jove, I will." In a flash my eager clinging lips were scattering passionate kisses all over Anna's bare knees. For a few moments she lay still and enjoyed with sensuous thrills the impetuous caress, until I, intent on exploring to effect my lustful object, slipped my hand up the smooth, satiny thigh.

I was getting uncomfortably near the coveted spot between her legs when Anna remembered what would happen if I got any further, cried out: "Stop, Gus Tolman, or I'll scream. You must not—go any further—I must not let you —you do it here." Her voice was soft and low, and she was panting and choking with her emotions.

My subtle touches and lustful kisses had burned deep in the impressionable, amorous young girl. She was just as passionate as I was and craved the same relief, but restrained herself through fear of possible consequences from yielding to passion's lure. She had the presence of mind to put off the longed-for pleasure. "Now, Gus, if you'll just wait until another time perhaps," she said. "No, no, Anna," I exclaimed with a fierce longing. "I must do it here—now —I can't wait, see how randy I am," I cried, and ripped open my trousers and produced my rampant penis. "Oh, Gus, I, too, can hardly wait, but I must. Why Gus, you'd surely make six babies in me with that lovely big thing. If you'll just wait until another time, I'll fix it so that we'll be safe."

"But," I cried, "we both love each other and we are so passionately hot, what can we do?" Anna was reclining on a rock with her arms outstretched and her loose silk waist was open revealing to my lustful gaze the deep dark crease between two lusciously full milky bubbies. It was a maddening sight to me.

"Come here, dear," said Anna, panting, her snowy bubbies heaving. "Come and kiss me, then I'll tell you what we can do." I threw myself on top of the billowy form and glued my mouth to hers in a long passionate kiss, then released her lips for the welcome plan.

"Darling," she said, "you know that I am terribly excited, too, and if you'll kiss me be—be—tween my legs, a nice long kiss with—with your tongue, you may do it in my—my bubbies."

This seemed such a strange and unnatural way to me to gratify passion, that I was amazed and gasped. "But Anna," I said, "I never did it that way. How can I gratify you with a kiss?"

"Let me have your mouth and I'll show you then," she replied. Then I once more pressed my lips to her and before I could think, she had thrust her nectarous tongue into my mouth, played it in and out, then wound it playfully about my own. Finally she sucked my lips between her teeth and tickled them with the tip of her tongue. I was almost frantic and Anna writhed and panted. "There, Gus, that's the way to kiss a girl between her legs. Only do it longer, dear, till I come. Oh, heavens, Gus, do it now. My pussy is so hot."

Anna had read all about such things in her father's medical library. When she observed me ready and eager to fulfill my part of the love feast, she very coquettishly pulled her dress up above her waist. The pink silk and lacy short open drawers were open wide so her snowy round belly and enticing sexual charm lay exposed in all its ravishing enticement before my lustful gaze. A silky, thick tuft of jet-black curls, like a fur cap, topped off the protruding thick ruby lips of her pussy jutting out with a saucy pout, between which I saw the dainty little crimson lips of the girl's salacious entrance to joys supreme. The black hair and pink drawers made a lovely contrast to the snowy flesh of Anna's white thighs and belly. This loving and naive introduction to her ravishing man-teasing charms made a lasting impression on me. With the lustful tenderness of a well-seasoned lover, I stooped and kissed the smooth belly from the waist down and all over, lingering awhile with my tongue digging in Anna's deep navel. She spread her legs apart more than ever for relief as my straying lips and tongue passed over her quivering belly. I knelt before the black-haired shrine pouting with erotic longing. Instantly, the beautiful girl placed her plump legs about my neck and sighed:

"Oh, Gus, kiss it." Parting the silky curls, I first kissed the soft pulpy lips lightly, then pressed my mouth against it and parted the lips with my tongue. That first taste and smell of a sweet delectable slit of a wholesome healthy woman made me madly infatuated with the strange act. The indescribably sweet flavor of a clean healthy woman "in heat" acted like a subtle nectar. The more I quaffed it, the more I wanted; for it sent my blood rioting through my body with a soul-stirring pulsation.

Like music, Anna's soft cries fell to my ears.

"Oh, dear, that's so nice." At that I thrust

my tongue into her very depths. Anna gave a smothered scream and exclaimed again: "Oh, my! Oh, my! How lovely!" Even if I had never been told what to do, my lustful mood would have prompted me. I worked my tongue in and out, sideways, and then way in until Anna moaned and writhed with the delightful sensation that it produced. My hands were caressing her belly and plump satiny bottom. Anna's breath was coming in short gusts, her belly heaved and she was speechless with ecstasy as her passions were nearing the climax. My tongue then found the ticklish clitoris and I played my tongue on it awhile, finally sucking it. Anna gasped and shuddered when her blissful joys came to an end. I heard the cries and soft moans:

"Oh—oo—Oh! Dar—ling—I'm com—ing, there—it—is." I felt her give down a warm gush of hot fluid on my clinging lips and tongue. As the girl's broken words and sighs came to me, softer and softer, I drew the whole of Anna's quivering thing into my mouth and sucked hard, continuing the magic tongue action till after a pause, Anna cried out: "Oh, darling, how entrancing, bring it again." I was enjoying with lascivious greed the salacious act and the unctious flavor of Anna's love-juice made me loathe to stop. Instinctively I began to lick and lap the inflamed lips of the soft juicy orifice. The girl's trembling legs tightened about my neck and she pressed both hands to my head and uttered agonizing cries: "Oh, Gus, you darling. It's—com—ing again—suck it—suck it—hard—Oh! My God! Gus—sie—I—I'm dy—ing."

I completed the orgasm with all the force I could apply. Anna laid shivering as she sank into a sea of ecstasy. I was now very eager for my relief. My prick was rigid and painfully swollen. Getting to my feet I tore off Anna's bust supporter that confined her voluptuous bubbies. I pushed down her waist. She squirmed out of it, and the lovely white shoulders and plump shapely arms, together with those firm milky breasts, surmounted by ruby nipples, was a maddening picture to me.

Rampant to the point of recklessness I had to struggle to keep from plunging my ferocious tool into the red swollen pussy that was still puckering and pouting with the effects of my lustful mouth action, but, consideration for Anna's safety and fear made me content with the prospect of relief as Anna had promised in her bubbies.

Altogether, it was a unique place to me and I was eager to try it as it looked extremely tempting. Anna had recovered her dazed senses and directed me to straddle her and placed my prick between her breasts. As I did so she held the soft warm yielding forms close about it. It was difficult to hold it snugly but she did it and cuddled it most lovingly. "Now, Gus you can do it and squirt the dangerous stuff on my neck," she said. The purple knob came near her ruby lips every time I jerked it back and forth in the pulpy, velvety enclosure. It wasn't long before I felt the climax coming. I cried out:

"Oh, Anna, this is lovely—it's—coming." She kept her eyes riveted on the highly inflamed and swollen knob as it moved in and out of the white flesh of her bubbies as she pressed them lovingly about the long shaft. I groaned and trembled, stopped moving and cried out: "Oh, God! there, Anna, see it—co—come."

The delicious sperm shot out in jets over her neck and ran down between her soft titties and shoulders. Quite fascinated, Anna had a sudden desire to complete my pleasure with her lips.

"Darling," she panted, "put it in my m-m-mouth." Her lips parted, and boldly and quickly she took the reeking knob, now relaxed, into her open mouth. She sucked it greedily till she had extracted the last drops of a long luscious spend. "Oh, Anna, darling, how I do love you," I cried out, "that was better than a real fuck."

When I helped my lovely amorous sweetheart from the rock, she clung to me and confessed in naive simplicity she never thought she could do what she had done, but because she loved me she could not help it. Although but twenty-one, Anna had all the mature thoughts and emotions of a much older woman. Reared in a free thinking atmosphere and given liberties few girls have, it was no wonder she gave a free rein to natural carnal passions, for she was alive and teeming with animal spirits and propensities.

As we strolled home that day, we frequently stopped in some secluded spot to indulge our amorous feelings in hugging and an exchange of passionate kisses and, before we parted it was agreed to meet on the following day and go to the same place where we had indulged in our first love desires together.

Anna was wise to the methods and expedients used by women to prevent conception. These she gleaned from medical books of her father's and always keen to observe the way certain women and girls dressed at receptions and on the street to lure men, Anna, with a cunning intent, devised and designed her own costumes to best set off her glowing and ravishing charms. For, well she realized she possessed physical charms that always attracted a libidinous gaze from me. So on the day she was to meet me again, she made herself alluring and tempting in a dress that not only set off her buxom, voluptuous charms, but revealed them as far as propriety permitted. A thin, white lawn waist showed her enticing, plump arms. Its rather low open front permitted a generous exposure of dazzling milky bubbies with that alluring valley from whence came a subtle odor of feminine sweetness.

A short skirt of blue flannel left Anna's handsomely formed legs molded in snug silk stockings. The low tan shoes accentuated her neat trim ankles. She was a vision to ravish any youth who was alive and appreciated the sensuously enticing charms of a woman.

I know that I trembled with rising lustful thoughts as I walked beside her. I was getting more and more inflamed and eager to indulge my amorous nature with this girl again. With cunning sagacity Anna had provided herself with a small safety sponge with a silk cord tied to it, and a small bottle of powerful antiseptic mixed with some vinegar. She knew that I would do it to her this time and so took the necessary precautions she had read of, namely, that if a woman saturated a small sponge and passed it up her vagina till it rested against her womb she could have sexual intercourse without fearing the consequences, for the liquid in the sponge would kill every drop of a man's spermy effusion, and both could still have their exquisite pleasures. Afterwards, she could withdraw the sponge with the dangerous juice dead in it. When we reached our love-tower beside the lake, Anna assumed the air of coquetry and pretended bashfulness. True to the nature of woman, Anna was a born tease and began tantalizing flirtations to further excite me. I was impatient.

The more I struggled to excite Anna's feelings and indulge in lover-like dalliance, the more she resisted, but my inflaming touches when I tried to fondle her only made the coquettish girl quiver with suppressed erotic emotion. Her blushes, dimples and the moist rosy lips revealed her real feelings. In my fury I managed to tip the girl back on the flat top rock and smother her with scorching kisses. She gasped, choked and struggled, just to tease me. By now I was furiously rampant and pulled her clothes up to her waist.

"Oh—oo—what a naughty boy you are today," she exclaimed. She was burning hot between her legs. That sudden uncovering of her sweet charms sent a thrill of intense passion through her. Thinking that she was cold to my advances and still had to be coaxed and tempted, upon seeing the plump, white flesh of her naked thighs and that maddening black-haired pussy, I buried my face in the black thick hair and thrust my tongue into the juicy slit. "Oh, Gus, not that way," said Anna, softly, "let me up—and—I'll do—do something."

I helped her off the rock. Then getting the sponge and bottle of antiseptic, she saturated the sponge, laid down on the bed of grass, pulled up her clothes, spread her thighs and worked the sponge clear up into her quivering pussy. I watched her with mingled feelings of amazement and lust as she explained the purpose of the strange act. Getting up, she flung her arms about me, and kissing me joyously, she purred:

"Now, Gus, I can be real naughty and let you do it to me."

I was rubbing my rigid tool against her thigh when she exclaimed: "Oh, Gus," as I held her close and thrust a free hand in her trembling bosoms and squeezed the velvety orbs. "Oh, Gus, let me see your lovely big thing." I drew back and opened my trousers. They glided to the ground, and then I kicked them off and pulled up my shirt and the overwrought girl gasped when she beheld the ferocious looking spear.

"Lay down, Anna," I commanded. Trembling with a certain fear and sexual excitement, she arranged herself on a grassy mound, tucking her dress well up under her back. Her bare bottom buried in the cool green grass with those beautiful silk-clad legs and delicately rounded thighs spread apart, she presented a voluptuous seductive feast of charms to be enjoyed by her lover.

I dropped between her slightly elevated knees and brought the turgid knob of my stiff and throbbing prick to the pulpy lips of her slit. As she looked up into my eyes she stammered:

"Gus, do be careful. You are the first one that ever did it to me." I quickly remembered when I seduced a virgin and asked her:

"Oh, Anna, are you a virgin?" to which she replied, "No, I don't think so, but its never been done to me before."

Believing her, I felt reassured and tenderly laid my bare belly on hers, my eager instrument poking about in the silky hair. Anna was a novice, but she was wise and thoughtful enough to reach down and guide her lover's impatient charger. The moment that I felt the throbbing hot orifice I pushed inch by inch on my way into the tight and luscious cunnie of the trembling, breathless girl.

"Ouch!—Oh!—My—big—lovely—boy—how it hurts," cried Anna, and carried away by her amorous feelings at her first sexual connection, she became oblivious to pain or fear.

How I did revel in the soft sensuous delights, for she was not only a delight to the eye but voluptuously appetizing to all other senses.

At first, following my developed skill in the sexual act, I did not hasten to spoil a long drawn-out enjoyment of this lovely fresh piece of femininity. With Anna, her desire and craving for relief made her wantonly eager for it. Intuitively she followed the dictates of animal passion. The itch for frictional excitement showed in her restless movements. She wriggled her buxom bottom and clung affectionately to me with winding arms and robust legs that impatiently tried to hold me closer. The bucking pussy of a beautiful passionate girl would have brought any normal young man to the melting point and climax, but I restrained myself to get out of this feast with Anna all the thrills and erotic sensations that I could.

With my tool sheathed and throbbing, I enjoyed, with the zest of a young connoisseur, the biting freshness of an unfucked pussy and titillation of possessing the glowing charm of such an amorous creature as Anna Burton. The intense and delirious enjoyment of her first fuck was shown in her heaving bubbies and undulating form, heavy breathing, and choking, gasping moans.

"Oh darling, Gus," she cried. "Isn't it lovely —Oh—it—feels—so—good—it doesn't hurt— Oh, Gussie, kiss me."

I glued my mouth to hers and thrust my tongue way into her mouth. She sucked it hard and gave a smothered scream, her eyes rolled, her pussy bucked, and I felt the entrancing spasmodic nips of her vagina and lovely hug of her smooth plump legs around my bare bottom. Anna's inaudible moans and choked cries punctuated those spasms of a long luscious spend. The voluptuousness of that entrancing experience with Anna's delirium of pleasure produced such lascivious and titillating thrills in me that I had to let fly a profuse spend. Heavens, what an ecstasy was ours. After a short but blissful die-away in which my tool soaked and welled in our mingled love-juices I was again rampant and eager for another. In my impatience I tore her waist entirely loose and pushed it off, leaving her snowy, velvety shoulders bare and those panting milky bubbies all exposed. How I sucked those stiff rosy nipples and her lovely shoulders and arms.

I was now moving my revived penis in and out, most entrancingly to Anna, when she cried out: "Stop, Gus dear, while I take the sponge out and fix it again." I released her and reluctantly arose while she drew it out with the silk cord, the sponge being laden with thick spend. Saturating it again with the medicine, she replaced it and lay back and said with a sweet smile:

"Now, darling, now for another—Oh, Gus, it's so lovely I could do it all day."

This time we revelled in a long drawn out feast that could never be described by Anna, for, hot and thrilled to the bone, she revelled in one orgasm after another till she lay exhausted. I had gone off quite often and was also drunk with extravagant spendings. After a while of unspoken, blissful joy in each other's arms we gradually recovered. I felt like a dip in the cool lake and told Anna I was going to strip and have a swim. Anna said that she would relish a dip but she could not swim. I peeled off her skin-tight stockings, caressing the plump, white smooth calves and fat dimpled knees. Anna was soon standing nude on the shore of the lake, quite safe from other eyes. She was a vision of rare loveliness and sensual beauty, and to me she was a constant stimulant to my sensual nature. I gazed long and hungrily on her shapely white form. It was perfectly proportioned and without the blemishes seen in most girls of her age. The black wavy hair and black tuft of curls on the protruding plump fullness of her cunnie made a most pleasing contrast to her white skin. I was enraptured. Our naked bodies were pressed together during an amorous feast of nectarous kisses which inflamed us afresh, but discretion prevailed for the moment and we proceeded to take a bath.

Anna was particular to remove and cleanse the sponge, which was well laden. Then we waded in the water and washed our sexual charms thoroughly. I swam for awhile as Anna waded about with bouncing springy bubbies appearing on the surface of the water. They were pretty enough to eat. I suddenly found I couldn't resist their alluring call to be fondled. We each felt and fondled the other until we were eager for another love feast.

I suggested having it under water, as a novelty. Anna recharged and replaced the sponge in her hot and quivering cunnie. I laid down on the sloping sandy beach with my hips and tool standing just under the water and directed Anna to sit astride of it. The girl's charming little slit was tighter than ever and clung firmly about my prick as she came down on it. The internal contact was hot and produced a thrilling contrast to the cooling waters outside. I was impressed with the titillating and deliciously ecstatic experience. I often have referred to it in my reminiscing as the most exquisite pleasure I have ever experienced—a fuck underwater.

Anna's lovely titties were free to fondle and gaze upon. I could not move, but Anna soon discovered a way to produce the frictional excitement she craved. She slowly and sensuously twisted her buxom bottom and moved up and down crying out: "Oh, Gus, isn't this a lovely way?—how good it feels in the water." Then becoming more and more excited, she discovered she could jerk her sheathing pussy convulsively up and down and thus give us both the heavenly delights we desired most. A delirium of sensuous thrills soon brought us to the climax of bliss. I clutched her tensely strained bottom and watched the twitching upward jerks of her cunnie and round, white belly. It acted like a pump and its vigorous suction brought me to the melting point amidst her groans and cries.

When she felt the knob burst and fill her vagina with scorching hot juice, she gave a scream, shuddered and with a hard bent back, she too went off with cries of ecstasy: "Oh, Gus—it's—com—ing—Oh, darling—Oh!"

Falling forward on me, Anna covered my

face with feverish, impetuous kisses, even biting me in her frenzy. With both hands holding and squeezing the hard cheeks of her bottom, I held the spending girl firmly to me in a blissful, rapturous die-away, both of us dizzy in joy. For a long time we luxuriated. The lake's waters lapped and splashed against the sensitive parts of us in the closest union. The titillating action of the water not only revived us but tickled and excited us with renewed lustful feelings and before we knew it, we were again swept into a sea of irresistible emotions that brought down another orgasm in which we both spent the last drops of exhausted lust.

We proceeded homeward in a dazed state of mind, but arranged for clandestine meetings when we would continue our youthful love-feastings. We indulged freely to the end of the summer vacation, when we departed for home. The amorous Anna was married soon after to a rich man and I lost all knowledge of her, but this affair with Anna Burton would never be forgotten.

PART TWO

It occurred to Mister Tolman one summer that a change of scene and rest might be beneficial and possibly afford him new amatory adventures. Hearing of a farmer and his wife who occasionally took summer boarders at their farm in the famous Catskill Mountains, he made arrangements to spend a month there.

On his arrival he found a gentle Dane, John Nolsen, by name, and his sturdy wife, and daughter Ollie. This family was scrupulously clean and orderly about their home and persons, but very lax as to morals and this fact was soon observed in their actions and conversations, which were often suggestive of lewdness.

Naturally little or no restraint was placed on the daughter, Ollie, a healthy, robust, attractive girl of nineteen. She was buxom, plump and rosy, bubbling over with health, radiating animalism and sexuality. With rosy cheeks, brilliant, plump lips, keen blue eyes, and a form that was matchless for its rich round development, Ollie Nolsen was indescribably handsome.

* * *

When I arrived I was attired in a natty golf suit, with its knee breeches and thin silk shirt displaying my own attractive (to women) figure and development to perfection.

Upon seeing me, Ollie became confused and highly excited, for as she said she had never seen such an attractive man before. Her eyes sparkled, her stiff buxom bubbies heaved with admiration and untutored lustful emotions and yet she was, in a way, piquantly modest.

All her animal spirit, carnal appetites and physical beauty seemed to burst into song. Passion was there as pronounced as in any lovely, amorous woman under restraint.

The mother was of the same type and nature and I contemplated both with longing eyes, but never betraying my secret thoughts. Both mother and daughter cast furtive eyes over me, taking in with quick perception my build and handsome face and heavy hung prominence in my trousers.

The husband and father was of medium build and had evidently lost his vigor, judging from the sad longing and regret shown in his wife's face. Presumably the pleasures due her were no longer obtainable, and surely she showed evidence of enough animalism to warrant any virile man a guess that she would welcome and relish a healthy, rollicking piece of vigorous manhood.

I quickly got into the graces of both women, who danced about with energy and feverish delight to make the new boarder feel comfortable and at home. I glared as their buxom charms came into reckless prominence as each woman flitted about, apparently showing off.

Ollie's handsome strong legs, revealing their attractive shape in white stockings, were visible to the knees, which were bare, their dimpled plumpness showing every time she turned quickly and her skirts flew up. I noted with lascivious alertness the gorgeous curves and voluptuous outlines of a handsome buxom rump, its soft round buttocks trembling with every step.

Amorous juice was rapidly filling my reservoir of sexual sweets and as I sat and made talk, getting acquainted, my ever perceptible penis was getting uncomfortably stiffer and bigger every moment. The mother's keen discerning eye saw and measured it. Stepping into the pantry (they were getting supper) she spoke in low tones and sighed: "Oh, Gott, Ollie, did you see his jock? Not much like our Papa's. Oh, Gott, it makes me feel young again."

The low-toned conversation was heard by Gus, who was alone, John having gone away from the house on some errand. Ollie answered her mother with excited quick breathing. "Of course I saw it Mamma, wouldn't it feel good?"

"Oh, Gott, Ollie you are too young to think of such things and you wouldn't appreciate such a man."

"Oh, Mamma," trembled Ollie, "I have longed for such a man for a lover ever since I was sixteen and I'm tired of using my fingers. I wonder if he likes us."

Then supper was ready and all sat down. I entertained the family with talks of my travels and an occasional risque story, which they seemed to relish and laugh heartily at. Smuttiness seemed to attract Mrs. Nolsen. Her eyes danced and her laughing countenance would flush with the warmth of renewed animal spirits as each story was related, each one getting more and more suggestive as I ran on. Mrs. Nolsen was a good looking woman of about forty and one who had retained her youthful freshness. She certainly looked good to me, for I thought her most appetizing and tempting with her shapely white arms bared and her opulent charms constantly coming into view in the loose open neck of her waist.

The father, John, enjoyed the stories and said that he was glad to have someone about to make the girls kittenish. "I wish I was young again," he remarked with a return of lickerish expression in his once sensual face. "I was a hot buck once, but when a man reaches fifty, he can't make the old fellow stand up for action any more."

They all laughed and the mother said that he shouldn't object to a young man like Mr. Tolman taking pity on a woman who was hungry for a good loving.

Ollie was all that the mother had been in her youth, passionate, lustful and delectable, and I judged the mother's capacity for sexual delights by all that the daughter suggested now.

After supper John retired to his paper while the women put away the dishes and afterwards he retired to bed leaving me to be entertained by the girls, as he called them. I found a large hammock on a vine-covered porch and was sitting in it when the women came out. I invited them to each sit in it beside me while I told them more stories and related my adventures. I was never a man who could resist temptations to indulge in amorous suggestive dalliance with two such sensuously alluring women so close. During my suggestive stories I placed an arm about their necks. My hands crept into the loose necks of their waists. The touch of soft velvet flesh and plump susceptible charms had an immediate effect on all three. I was getting rampant. Both girls were getting frisky and perceptibly enjoyed my open flatteries. I slowly withdrew my right hand from Anita's soft milky bubbies, tipped the unsuspecting

Ollie back and glued my mouth to hers. It was moist and luscious. "Ah, my lovely luscious girl," I exclaimed. "You are delicious, beautiful, passionate," and at the same time my free hand was shoved up under her dress and up along her lovely smooth bare knees and thighs. I squeezed the firm buxom buttock while my other hand continued to mold and toy with the impressionable girl's luxurious bubbies.

With a gasp and perhaps fear or mock modesty, she began to resist my advances and muttering in whispers: "Not here—not now—Oh, Mister Tolman, I'm afraid—you—must not. Father may come." In her struggle to free herself, her free hand came in contact with my hard stiff penis which was almost bursting in my trousers. She gave it a squeeze. It almost went off. "Oh, Gott!" her mother cried, "shame on you. You ought to behave." The mother was apparently jealous and in a sudden impulse she retired, first asking me when I desired breakfast.

I explained that I wanted fruit served in my room at five. I really had a motive as I generally awoke at that time with an uncomfortable hard-on and figured that one or the other of the women would fetch it.

Of course I had withdrawn my hand and when Mrs. Nolsen arose and said good-night and warning her daughter to behave herself and be careful, she disappeared. I got so rampant and of course followed up my chances. Ollie became even more amorous as I continued to make ardent love to her. She yielded to my lips and fondling of her plump shoulders and heaving firm bubbies.

"Call me Gus," I said to her as I rubbed my

stiff penis, confined within my trousers, up against her robust thigh. "Oh, Gott, you make me crazy," she exclaimed, as she writhed in my arms.

In a moment of excitement, when her dress had worked up to her knees, I gazed at a pretty pair of legs. Although sturdy and firmly modeled, they were beautifully shaped, tapering down to slender ankles and pretty feet. I couldn't resist. I passed my hand with deliberate libidinous caresses up and down the firm rounded calf and up over the smooth dimpled knees (she wore no drawers), going a little higher each time. Finding a vulnerable nerve, which when caressed, made the amorous girl cuddle and breathe rapidly, I poured out inflaming flattery.

"Ollie, darling, you were made for me—you make me crazy—may I touch it—feel it? Fondle your little cunt—your love-nest between your legs," I panted to her.

"Oh, Gott, Gus, I should not. I never let a man do that before and we might get too naughty."

The girl's naive talk was piquant and alluring. I tried to force a hand between the bare legs she held so tightly shut. "Feel mine, girlie," I said. Already bereft of all modesty, a small plump hand stole slowly to my swelling penis, which was heaving and throbbing with pulsating lust. "Oh, Gott," cried Ollie. "It's so big——I—I—never saw one like it. I've only seen Papa's and boys', and they are so small. Papa's is never stiff like yours." Gradually her thighs parted. My hand crept between them. Ollie was squeezing the turgid monster.

With a gasp the buxom girl sank back on the

couch and I with her as she impulsively spread her legs apart, as if inviting the searching hand. I quietly clasped a thick bunch of silky hair and a soft pair of thick lips. My middle finger searched and found a tight puckering orifice. She was speechless, but her short tumultuous breathing showed how she was affected. I strained her to me in a passionate embrace, kissed and sucked the delicious moist mouth and jabbed my finger into her quivering cunnie up to the knuckle and held her tightly in my grasp.

Ollie trembled, and murmured in a soft thick voice, "Oh, Gott, it's com—ing—Mister Goos." She suddenly relaxed and melted softly in my arms and gave my penis a terrific squeeze as I felt a gush of warm creamy spend wet my fingers and palm. I was frantic to gratify my own lustful feelings but did not hasten matters for fear of being repulsed. I did not relinquish my hold but kept up a flow of lascivious love-making and titillating finger action. I quickly discovered that Ollie had lost her virginity by the use of her fingers or other unnatural means in gratifying her girlish passions.

I got a salacious delight in testing the firm, rubber-like lips and elastic orifice of Ollie's succulent, healthy young cunt and when I rolled the stiff hard clitty between my thumb and finger she began to writhe. Her amorous passions were again kindled and she didn't appear to care what happened. She became reckless and abandoned herself to the alluring sensations a real man had brought to her lonely life and erotic nature. When I tipped Ollie back till she lay prone upon her back and told her to open her legs, she offered no resistance. It was now dark so she did not see or notice me open and lower my trousers, or that my rampant penis was bared and ready for action. I leaned over the buxom, amorous girl and taking her in one arm, I guided my penis and worked the turgid knob up and down between the elastic lips.

Feeling that it was at the tight puckering hole, I glued my mouth to her lips to smother her possible cries and pushed hard. The head slipped in and Ollie tried to scream. Then, with one vigorous shove I sent the full eight inches to the hilt. I found the way deliciously tight, but lusciously well lubricated. Lying still, to let her get accustomed to the stretching, I enjoyed with lustful zest the lovely plump shoulders and firm springy bubbies. I pushed her loose waist down and passing a caressing hand over the velvety skin, I whispered appealingly to her, "Oh, Ollie, you are a deliciously lovely girl to fuck."

Ollie, like most country girls, quickly caught on to the vulgarisms and suggestive expressions, using her own naive way of saying them, adding a touch of Danish language which made her all the more fascinating. As the first pain of the brutal insertion passed and Ollie experienced those delightful thrills produced by the big tool of a virile man, she moaned:

"Oh, Gott, how lufly it feels to be foocked." Goaded by intense passion and desire to get as much of the man as possible, she wound her lovely fat legs around me and strained me to her with wanton force and amid gurgling expressions. "My cunt—luffs it—Oh, Gott! Oh, Gott it's lufly." I now began a slow in and out stroke, increasing in speed till the lively friction brought down a second frenzied spend for her.

She wanted to scream, but I smothered her with passionate kisses and filled her mouth with my tongue, but her moans, groans, heaving bosom, and strong clutchings all expressed the joy and ecstasy of the girl's first experience with a man. The stolen bliss, darkness, and moonlight sifting through the vines, together with the exquisite pleasure of being the first man to have her, lifted me to a pinnacle of agonizing thrills.

In soft tones I told her of my feelings as the climax came to my frantic feast: "Ollie—your's is a lovely cunt—I'm com—ing—I'll—fuck—you — full—of—love-juice—there—there—take — that and that—Oh! feel me—come—there!"

She closed her eyes and fell back in a swoon as the limpid, creamy sap gushed forth and struck her thirsty womb. As we died away in a ravishing bliss, the girl gurgled, "Ach, Himmel—Ick—Sturbe."

I arose from her and told her to stand up and pee to wash out the dangerous juice. She did this. I then told her to squirt some vinegar up her little cunt before she retired to kill any juice that might be left in her.

I spent the night in lascivious dreams in which buxom female charms and fleshy indulgences tantalized me. It was a few minutes before five the next day when I awoke with my usual morning erection, made more ferocious by the experience of the night before, the memory of which still lingered.

John had gone to the barn to milk and do the other chores until called for breakfast at seven-thirty. Ollie was fast asleep in another room, when her mother attired in nothing but a loose wrapper, proceeded to place the fruit in my room. She had not dressed, merely throwing on a wrapper, fully intending to complete her toilette later.

Nita rapped at my door. As the night had been very warm I had retired naked. I had kicked the sheets off and when I heard the summons, I did not answer, suspecting one or the other of the women would fetch the fruit. I pretended to be asleep. Nita opened the door softly, and stepped in. The sight that met her half awake eyes and senses made her drop the fruit. I was peeking out of one eye. I then stirred as if suddenly awakened. My amorous penis was standing up magnificently proud, splendidly inflamed and nodding majestically.

The woman let out a scream of surprise and consternation, her eyes almost popping out of her head as she gazed in wonder at the stately affair with its purple knob and tightly wrinkled bag hanging snugly at the lower end.

The profusion of brown kinky curls covering the bag and half way up the shaft, spreading thickly over my belly was a thrilling sight to Nita, who was unaccustomed to any such specimen of a man's sexual organ. She seemed for a moment dazed and then fascinated. One hand went to her eyes and the other to her opulent breasts. She gasped. Her breath came in gusts, her nostrils dilated, her eyes flashed, then became languorous. I heard a low almost indistinguishable moan.

"Oh, Gott, if I only dared. How grand. How goot it would feel. Oh, Gott forgive me. I must." The splendid tempting morsel kept trembling and nodding. "Ach, my Gott! it's alive." I stirred and then opened my eyes and gazed at the panting woman, trembling with intense passion, as I spoke to her:

"Ah, Nita—how good of you to come. You are not frightened, I hope. Come," I said, stretching out my arms. "Come, you need it."

"Ach, yes, Mister Tolman, I—I—do," she cried in a hungry manner. "You won't tell? Ach Himmel, how I want it."

"Take off your gown Nita!" I said in a commanding voice. Slowly the dazed woman proceeded to slip off her gown. Her face was profuse with a glow of blushes. Her gown fell to the floor and I feasted my eyes on a form that was matchless in perfect symmetry and beautiful contour. Nothing had marred the superbly matured form of what was once a young girl of supreme beauty with lines and curves suggesting Venus. Every inch of the handsome figure seemed to bubble over with radiant health. Rich, round, strong bubbies, full to bursting, seemed eager to spurt jets of passionate milk from their stiff outstanding nipples. An alluring tuft of flaxen curls shaded the plump prominent mound in which appeared a deep slit between the protruding fat lips, opening and closing with that throbbing pulsation found only in vigorous manifestations of an animal in heat. But when she turned to lock the door, I beheld the most ravishing handsome white bottom, rippling with dimples in the trembling flesh, that I ever hoped to see. Like two abnormally large flushing peaches, her buttocks stuck out impudent and buxom. "Good God," I exclaimed, "come here quick, Nita, I must have that gorgeous voluptuous bottom."

She rushed to the bed and fell on me with a gasp and groan. Her pulpy red lips kissing every inch of that towering weapon she craved. She almost devoured it. I reached out and drew the famished woman to my side and she clung to me as a hungry hound to a piece of meat.

I at once bounded on top of her. Instinctively Nita wound her beautiful well-shaped limbs about me.

"Ach, man, foock me, foock me to death. It's the first I've had in years," she cried. I made up my mind to give the beautiful Mrs. Nolsen a treat she would not soon forget. I got into a position from which I could operate in a way to afford her pleasure and produce voluptuous sensations but could thoroughly enjoy the sensuous banquet of flesh, so wantonly and unexpectedly thrown my way. I lewdly fondled her delectable charms most greedily. Taking my penis in one hand, I worked its knob between the elastic fat lips of one of the most adorable pussies I had ever had. The action and manipulation of Nita's firm milky bubbies and their stiff red points inflamed her to a pitch of frenzy. When my tool was well lubricated I inserted the plum-shaped head in the puckering, quivering orifice and pushed.

Never before feeling anything so large, the woman squealed and exclaimed: "Ach, Gott, how lufly it hurts. Put it all—all in me."

I got well on top of the buxom form, drew her fat legs up over my hips and with one ferocious shove buried it to the hilt.

Sheathed in a hot clinging vigorous nest, I experienced sensations which few women ever afforded me. This woman, hot and overwrought with sexual desire, yielded quickly to the voluptuous sensations. The pulsations of the big knob held firmly against her womb sent her blood boiling and she was speechless with ravishing delight. Her eyes rolled and her lips quivered. She groaned, the groans coming quicker and quicker rose to cries, and then I got the full meaning of a woman's joy, denied and starving for the delights of the flesh.

"Oh, Gott in Himmel," she gurgled, "I—I—coom."

Only the whites of her eyes showed; her face, distorted with the agony of intense erotic pleasure was a picture of lust that pleased me. Her frenzied orgasm made her tremble and quiver. I felt each spasm in her pulsating womb and the ferocious nipping all along my penis. Nita sank into a blissful languor, and I then began a slow in and out action to produce the friction that we both wanted. It soon produced another ecstatic orgasm for her, this time a little less frenzied, but long and sensuous. Another followed in close succession. The poor woman was hungry for it and took all the delightful sensations she could get, finally saying in a voice and words choking with emotion: "Oh—you—wonderful—man—why—you—not—coom. I want to—f—feel—you coom."

"Yes, my dear," I said, as I continued to thrust with greater energy. "I'll come now—now." I slipped her legs down and folded her in my arms and began to thrust harder than ever. "There—there—Nita—there, how heavenly I spend." I then shot delicious spermy juice in a long thick stream, the spending of which made her see stars; it was intensely ecstatic. In a half-dazed condition I raised up and spoke flatteringly in a way that made the poor woman smile through her tears of agonizing pleasure. "Oh, Nita, I never fucked such an adorable woman, you are too lovely for words—God, how tight and delicious."

She faintly replied: "Oh, Mister Tolman, you are the lufliest man. Oh, Gott, why hasn't my man got one like yours, eet ees so long, so beeg and it makes me come so lufly. Oh, Gott in Himmel, you are so stiff yet."

"Yes—yes, my lovely Nita, you keep it stiff with your adorable cunt, it bites so nice. Put your legs together when I raise up—so, that's fine," I said, as she brought her fat thighs together, imprisoning my long thick tool in her tight box flooded with hot juice. "Now, dear girl, I'll treat you to one that you'll not forget."

"Oh, Gott, I'll never forget the first one," she cried. It was now nearly six o'clock and I knew that the woman had to be downstairs soon, so I began an irresistible, long, deep pushing, my strong limbs squeezing hers together in a passion that was devouring. My hips flew up and down producing a friction of parts that made us both maudlin. The piston-like strokes brought us both to an ecstatic climax. I sank down on the hard springy, upstanding bubbies, groaned, and let fly my fresh store of sap. "Oh, Gott, vee coom—to—get—ter," cried Nita, as her tightly crammed cunt strained and sucked my bursting penis. It never stopped until the woman, frantic with voluptuous delight had sucked two juicy spends in delirious succession from me. It was all I could do to pull my spent tool from the clinging lips and walls of Nita's gorged and satisfied cunt.

I revived her with a drink of brandy, taking one myself. She arose and almost tottered as she drew on her wrapper and the thick stream of spend ran down her thighs. She never spoke but went below. I quickly dressed. As I started down I saw Ollie ahead of me. I didn't speak but went on slowly. Ollie rushed into the kitchen and seeing her mother's bright red cheeks, heavy languorous eyes and happy smile she stopped and suddenly exclaimed:

"Why, Mamma, what has happened to you? You look as if you had been drinking or were drunk. What makes you look so happy?"

"Hoosh, hoosh, Ollie, I am drunk—drunk with —man, I am—Oh, so happy—I feel—like—a colt. Oh, Gott, Ollie, don't ever tell. I've been in bed with him, the new man."

"Heavens, Mamma," cried Ollie, "I'll never tell, he—he foocked me last night. Isn't he just grand. Gott, I could let him do it every night."

"Gott help uns," cried the mother, "I believe you have a baby."

"Oh, no, Mamma, he told me what to do— I washed it all out."

I overheard all and saw them. Nita's face was a study at Ollie's sudden confession. After that they became very confidential and acted like two chummy thieves.

Each helped the other to indulge in making plans in their new found pleasure. I ate my breakfast alone. Both women waiting on me with vivaciousness and wanton flaunting of their opulent charms as they moved about. I said to them that I would spend the day hunting in the woods. That same evening I learned that John and Nita would go early the next morning to the city to shop and attend to some business and would leave Ollie behind to prepare my meals.

Ollie and I spent the evening together in the hammock, making love to each other and indulging our amorous feelings in fondling and toying. We made plans to spend the following day when we would be alone, in bed together. I wished to conserve my energies and love liquor so we refrained from indulging in anything more suggestive than kisses, feelings and fingerings. Ollie got so randy and hot that she begged me to fuck her just once with my big doddle, as she liked to call it, but I desisted, saying that I would give her all that she wanted the next day. "Ach, man," she murmured, "you are not a real man if you won't foock me or make me feel good with your finger." I had the girl's waist half off and her snowy bubbies exposed. I sucked them and kissed them all over, sucking the cockish stiff nipples, at the same time molding her thighs and bottom with sensual motions. I never missed such a chance.

Toying with a pretty plump woman always kept me in a highly charged condition for prolonged fleshy indulgences with my passions. With a husky passionate young woman like Ollie Nolsen in the full flesh of animalism and knowledge of sexual powers it was different. She radiated hot longings, and bubbled over with amorous passion and youthful lust. In her desires to be fucked, she became maudlin. She tore open my trousers and ferociously drew out my turgid penis. With an impulse born of wild lust she fell on it like a hound to a bone and kissed it all over. She lipped it and tried to get the head into her mouth. It was too large. She toyed with the hard wrinkled balls and gurgled: "Oh you beauty, I could eat you." Her strong hands squeezing and manipulating, together with her clinging mouth, almost made me spend. I pushed her off and laid her back. She thought that I was about to mount her, when I suddenly dropped to my knees. I pushed her dress up and pressed the soft fat thighs apart and gazed on her by the light of the moon. I noted a delicious savory odor of the young woman's heat. It was enticing. I knew that she was clean and wholesome and was quickly convinced that she was delectably kissable between her legs. I concluded to introduce her to the French kiss. Of course she had never heard of such a thing and when I lightly kissed the lips of her pouting pussy she gave a little gasp and cry:

"Oh, Mister Gus, who ever heard of kissing a girl there?"

"Wait, Ollie dear," I replied, "you'll like it—I'm going to fuck you with my tongue." Again she gasped and exclaimed, "Oh, my Gott."

I lavishly kissed along her thighs and belly, and the pouting lips of her soft slit. I pulled them apart and buried my mouth in the juicy meat. Ollie quivered, gave little gasps and almost screamed when I ran my tongue into the tight orifice and wriggled it around. I enjoyed the succulent freshness of her lovely, young pussy with a keen relish. It was so different from any of those that I had ever kissed before. It was so tight and passionately warm. When I did get my tongue all the way in and rubbed my teeth against the protruding clitty the surprised girl jerked up her prominent mound in convulsions of hot longing.

I heard the soft moans increase to little gasping cries: "Oh—Oh—Goos, that's so—lufly—Oh, dear, it's—it's coming." Her lovely fat legs were entwined about my neck, and her thighs closed tight against my head and face and held me in a convulsive grip when her orgasm came.

In her spending spasms her vagina sucked hard on my tongue. It was ferocious. Ollie's little drops of spurting juice, warm from her womb, moistened my tongue and before the spend was complete, I withdrew my tongue and, drawing the puckered orifice with its throbbing lips into my mouth, chewed and sucked like mad. Ollie fainted and cried: "Oh, Gott, it's—it's com—ing again—Oh, it's—so—good!"

The long gurgling groans bespoke the girl's ecstatic pleasure. I eagerly lapped up the girlish sap. Her legs loosened and fell away as she swooned in a faint. I took her in my arms and whispered, "Ollie, dear, I never kissed such a sweet adorable pussy in my life."

She replied in a voice faint and low, trembling with passionate emotions: "Will you kiss me that way again?"

"Yes, dear, tomorrow." After she recovered we both prepared to retire. She paused before going upstairs to say:

"Goos, I am so glad that you gave Mamma a nice time this morning. Poor Mamma, she never gets it any more. They leave on the first train at six in the morning."

I was up to see Ollie's parents off. Nita managed to get a word with me, telling me to be careful and not get Ollie in the family way, and to Ollie she said:

"Be careful and do what Mr. Tolman tells you. He knows what to do."

Ollie had dressed most attractively for me. Leaving off troublesome drawers and corsets she wore a short-skirted dress with a sleeveless waist so loose and open, her gorgeous young bubbies betrayed their rounded forms with every movement. The short skirt revealed her handsome rounded legs and bare dimpled knees, a pair of black silk stockings setting off alluringly the pink and white smooth flesh of her legs and thighs. She was justly proud of her youthful charms and displayed her pride in showing them before my ogling glances.

After she had put away the breakfast things, she stood before me and throwing her head back with a saucy smile and puckering lips and throwing out her plump impudent bubbies, she temptingly said:

"Come, kiss your poosy." With eyes shining and a sudden upward pull of her skirt, she flashed in bewildering wantonness her fluffy pussy. The picture goaded me. I sprang forward and almost crushed the girl in a mad passionate embrace and glued my mouth to hers, our tongues meeting.

With my usual morning hardon I was now so rampant that my prodigious tool poked the girl's belly and alert pussy. It made her randy and hot for it. We didn't tarry long but locking up the house we went to my room. There was a large mirror on my dresser which I arranged to reflect onto the bed. Quickly undressing, I laid down. When Ollie saw all this she tore her clothes off in hot haste and showed herself with innocent wanton boldness in lascivious alluring poses. I gloated and feasted my eyes on the nude form of the most beautifully shaped young woman ever I beheld. The curving back, dimpled and white, melted into round, saucy buttocks that stood out plump and soft; the baby-like flesh rippling and its pretty dimples aquiver with tingling lust.

On down my eyes swept to the beautifully rounded swelling hips and symmetrical thighs, melting in rounded knees full of dimples, and a pair of legs and ankles that were matchless in graceful curves. Her bubbies were remarkably lovely and exquisitely molded, with their ruby buds so strong and buxom. My inflamed penis bounded and throbbed. Every muscle in my body was tense with passion. Ollie threw herself onto me and devoured me with kisses and hands in her eagerness to possess me. I crushed the husky form to me in a mad embrace, enjoying lustfully the girl's caresses. She said:

"You handsome man, you must kill me—fuck me—to—death—Oh, do—it now," cried the impassioned girl. "Keep it in me all day."

I pinched the springy flesh and slapped and squeezed Ollie's hard buxom bottom. It cringed under my sharp stinging slaps, and the more and harder I slapped, the more maudlin and lustful she got.

I finally rolled her over and fondled her lovely bubbies and squeezed her fat juicy slit. She was panting with animal passion. I got over her and told her to put her legs over my back. Her thighs were thus stretched apart. "Put it in for me, girlie," I said. She had some difficulty in holding the rampant weapon. It kept springing out of her hand. She finally, with much laughter, got the head in the right place. I shoved, and with much groaning and some excruciating pain produced by the difference in size and strength, finally got it all in.

"Does it hurt?" I asked.

"Ah, it hurts good—don't—stop—shove—it—way—up—in—my—belly—Oh—Goot—I cum—lufly—Oh, God, I could die." I had finally buried my penis, and its throbs had touched her off. Not until her blissful state of ecstasy had subsided and she came, too, did I indulge my own erotic feelings in those frictional movements that thrill one. Ollie's tight little box had contracted so that I had difficulty in moving in and out, so I got both arms around the roly-poly bunch of sweetness, glued my mouth to her moist pulpy lips, then concentrated my virile, passionate strength and flowing magnetism. The soft velvety flesh yielded to my straining arms as they crushed into its sensitive liveliness. I knew that I was hurting the girl, for with every convulsive hug my tool expanded and she gasped and choked.

"Am I hurting you, darling?" I said. "Oh, Gott, yes, but don't stop. Every time you hurt I have that lufly feelings."

My penis was now gliding in and out with slow sensual lubricity that sends thrills and chills all through a man and a woman. Ollie was exquisitely voluptuous. Her legs slipped down and were wound about my limbs holding me in a hungry grapple. I tingled down to my toes, which seemed to curl up. My scalp was creepy, my hair felt as if it was curled up into kinks. Each thrust of my penis was met by a snappy jerk of Ollie's frenzied pussy. I yielded to the luxurious sensuous thrills. I know that I bellowed and yelled—

"Oh—Oh—Ollie, I'm—com—ing!"

Almost crushing the poor girl with a brutal crunching of bones, I exploded with prolonged sensuous stirring of lustful appetites, the pent-up sap overflowed, and long rich creamy spurts gushed from my belching pego in a delirium of thrilling spasms.

"Ollie," I exclaimed, "feel it come. God, how

ravishing—how lovely you are—that's right—suck the juice out of me—suck you beauty—Ah! Oh!—come—you—hot—little—cunnie."

Ollie screamed and expired in a swoon of delirious ecstasy. Gasping and panting we sank back into a sea of bliss that lasted for an hour in which our bodies were in contact, and conveying to each other amorous congeniality and sympathy, soon recovered our lustful desires for each other.

The firm mellow flesh of Ollie's buxom arms folded in the arms of a virile strong man, whose hard firm flesh imparted sexual power and vigor, again aroused in her, fresh longings for further indulgences. My amorous caresses and magnetic touches on highly sensitized nerves in the unsophisticated girl made her itch and burn for more sexual pleasure. Her amorous passions prompted her to a wanton indulgence of eroticism.

She displayed a keen lustful interest and joy in examining my sexual splendors. How she did toy with that abnormal love-giver. How she giggled when her manipulations of the tightly wrinkled balls and thick chubby mass of impressionable penis made it swell. How her eyes sparkled, and how she blushed when she took the soft pulpy head in her mouth, rolling her tongue around it, lovingly, till it expanded and hardened. Her soft moist lips, slipping it in and out of her distended mouth, maddened me into a fury of lust. I gloated over the succulent sweet lasciviousness of her husky little cunt, which snapped open and shut with lustful longings.

"Let's try a new position, Ollie," I said. "You get over me with your face towards my feet and your handsome big bottom over my face."

She laughed and eagerly complied. When I beheld the most adorable and fascinating rump I had ever seen, I was lavish with profuse admiration. Passing my hands, feverish with lust, over the smooth, white surface of her big buxom bottom that looked like a full moon in its complete roundness, I exclaimed with carnal lust: "Ye Gods, Ollie, what a gorgeous bottom, I must kiss it." Pulling the girl up, I kissed the velvety flesh of both cheeks. Then pulling the cheeks apart as far as I could, I lewdly kissed the bottom of her cunnie with deep thrusts of my tongue. It was clean and sweet, for Ollie had thoroughly cleansed herself before getting into bed.

Between the fat cheeks bulged the pouting lips of Ollie's adorable slit framed in light brown silky curls. The juicy inner lips protruded red and meaty, glistening with lubricity. I tickled them with my tongue. Ollie was lipping and tonguing the knob of my now turgid tool. "Oh, Goos, can't I have it now?" she pleaded.

"Gee, yes," I answered. "Move down." I held my tool in my hand and worked the purple knob between the soft lips and when Ollie felt the hot post at the entrance, she dropped heavily on the massive weapon. The passionate girl groaned and shook her big voluptuous rump, then settled down sheathing my whole eight inches with a greedy gulp. What a sensuous picture I had before me as I saw the crimson flesh of a succulent hot cunt clinging greedily about my tool like an elastic band, sucking to get more. In the mirror I watched the curving back and voluptuous bottom undulate in a spiral twisting movement to produce the friction that the lustful girl craved.

I caressed and spanked the round white cheeks and drew them apart that I might watch the lips of her cunnie clinging to my throbbing affair. What a lascivious picture it was to my gloating eyes. How I did shiver and wallow. I felt that I had never experienced anything quite so ravishing to my lustful nature. Ollie's pointed titties were tickling my knees with their rosy points. She crooned and gurgled her lustful efforts to please both of us and goaded herself on like a lash. Her sucking, pinching cunnie rose and fell, increasing in speed till the friction brought her passions to a climax. She screamed and shook her beautiful rump and buried her face between my legs and moaned. I felt the short spasm of the spending womb, the throbbing nips, and the girl's hot love essence squirt around my sheathed penis. As the gratified Ollie lay prone with my joy-giver buried deep in her, I exclaimed, "My God, how good it is—I—come—Oh—Oh!"

After a blissful die-away, we went to the bathroom where we relieved ourselves and then returned to dress. Ollie put on a youthful dress extending only to her knees to give me plenty of opportunity to watch her legs. She then put on red silk stockings. Under this pretense of a dress she wore nothing, having planned to give me as much freedom as possible. We got dinner together when I sought every opportunity to feel and fondle lustfully the lovely velvety charms of the buxom lass. In fact I had my hand on the big plump bottom most of the time, occasionally getting my fingers into the juicy slit. Both of us were in a constant state of lustful desire. While Ollie waited for dinner to cook she came to where I was sitting on a kitchen chair. I slipped my hands up and down the silky legs and handsomely formed thighs, spanking the elastic cheeks of her lovely buttocks. Her dress was open and the full round globes of her snowy bubbies were impudently thrust in my face. I sucked the saucy red tips. I was well primed for another go at the girl, and she was as hot as a blister. I wore only a light bathrobe, and my penis was erect and throbbing. "OO—oo," ejaculated Ollie, looking down at it. "Let's do it now." I was keen to have a piece on the chair, so I told her to straddle me, which she did, after removing her only raiment.

I feasted my eyes on the voluptuous vision for a moment where Ollie's mound was prominent and swollen. The lips were thick and pouting with lustful sensations. She was a lovely specimen of vigorous, burning passion. I clasped her hips and buttocks in my arms and drew the palpitating girl over my lap as she parted her beautiful thighs. Guiding my tool I inserted the knob in her juicy quivering notch. Supported on her feet she carefully let herself down deliberately and carefully, her eyes swimming in lust. Little cries escaped the impaled girl as she wriggled herself down and sheathed the long thick penis. With both hands I molded the firm round buttocks, and enjoyed with thrilling zest this position for I could bury my face in the velvety bubbies and suck the stiff red nipples. The caress of her smooth round belly and the mingling of the hair was exquisitely titillating.

"Oh, Goos," cried Ollie, "Oh—it's—so—goot. It's com—com—ing!" My penis was throbbing against her quivering womb, when she suddenly fell forward and glueing her red mouth to mine, spent with moans. I prolonged the sensuous enjoyment of Ollie with lickerish delight. When she came and felt the tormenting itch for friction in her inflamed tight cunnie she began to move up and down and twist and wriggle her buxom bottom, imparting sensations that made both her and myself maudlin. I groaned and writhed. The deliciously sensuous action of her nipping and sucking cunt was so delightful I could not resist nature's impulse. I bellowed. My toes curled. Thrills of exquisite sensations made me tremble: "Oh how—you—can—fuck! —There—there—it comes!" The limpid delirious sap shot into Ollie's ravenous box with creamy, unctuous spurts that made me see stars. Ollie screamed and trembled prettily as she, too, went off, her warm girlish juices mingling with my own balsamic effusion.

After a long blissful ecstasy, folded in each other's arms, we came to. Ollie raised herself and let the spent penis slip out. Our combined juices ran out of her inflamed and snapping pussy and fell in a puddle on the floor. It looked like pearly cream on the dark floor. Ollie gazed long at it, and then with a lickerish expression, softly spoke:

"Oh, Goos, my darling—I'd luff to taste that stuff—it made me coom so nice. Oh, Gott, it was lufly. Could you coom in—in my mouth?" quivered the girl with a sensuous smile.

"Why yes, Ollie dear, if you'll try. We'll suck each other off this afternoon."

After this we ate dinner in the nude. I never before had such a memorable meal in my life. Ollie was voluptuous and delectable as we sat opposite with her adorable titties and nude charms so sensuously exposed.

After dinner we again went to my room and spent the afternoon in bed. To me, having a pretty, adorable, fresh young damsel like Ollie Nolsen with me and time to burn, was a feast of sensuousness, rarely if ever enjoyed by the average man.

A delectable female, affectionate and amorous, with a form so deliciously perfect was a sharp stimulant to me, whose lustful appetites and poignant desires were for the moment dulled after freely indulging. Ollie, like any vigorous sexually strong and amorous young woman who had tasted the joys of voluptuous intercourse with a powerfully magnetic man who fascinated her, was true to nature, a seething furnace of unquenchable erotic passion. She toyed and played with me like a healthy young pup with a mastiff. She cuddled my penis in her velvety bubbies. She took the soft pulpy mass in her mouth, lipping and chewing it gleefully and hungrily. The contact of her cool flesh, soft and smooth as a baby's, the thick tuft of silky curls on a plump swelling mound, the glorious thighs, shapely legs, and plumply dimpled knees all afforded me a subtle titillating aphrodisiac. My testicles were again filled with a fresh sap in the making, while Ollie's efforts were rewarded with my abnormally large penis standing proudly magnificent and eager. The delighted girl cried out, in her impulsive eroticism:

"Oh, Goos, my beautiful lover, you are so beeg and stiff, give it to me again and make me hot and foock me hard."

"Ah, Ollie," I exclaimed, "you are the most fascinating and loveable girl I ever knew. How would you like to be my wife and mistress?"

The girl gasped: "Oh, Mister Tolman," she exclaimed, "I—I could never leave Mamma—let me think about it."

I folded the ravishing girl into my arms and said in a low, passionate voice: "Come, girlie, lie on your back, open your legs and give me your perfect cunt, and I'll give you my cock." Ollie quickly got onto her back, spread her lovely white thighs apart and presented her passionate pussy. This time she instantly took my sturdy penis in her hand and guided it to her quivering slit. I plunged and buried the well-primed tool to the hilt and worked it firmly in and out. Resting on my hands I gazed lustfully on Ollie's pretty face and into her limpid blue eyes, swimming in mists of passion. I could also feast my eyes on her beautiful bubbies turbulent with emotion. I felt the clasping of her passionate thighs as the lively friction produced by my rapid thrusts caused intense sexual excitement. Ollie's moans and cries with each spasm of ecstasy was music to me in my taste for sensuousness. The prolonging of my lustfulness and enjoyment goaded the emotional and passionate girl into a fury of repeated orgasms. She fairly wallowed in her ecstatic screaming every time, as I molded a plump bubbie in my hand and strained my prodigious penis against her passionate womb.

"Oh, my lover," she finally groaned, "give me the juice." I then let it fly. It shot with hot force into her depths. "'Juice," she groaned, coming once more. "Oh—that's—so—good—I could die—don't—take—out."

We rolled over and over convulsed with bestial lust and when the lovely form of the girl was on top I glanced into the mirror and gloated on the undulating, writhing contours of her handsome bottom, rising and falling in her eagerness for frictional action.

It was a sensual picture, that I never forgot. In a storm of love cries and smothered screams and straining bodies we both dissolved and melted away in a swoon of ecstasy.

After a long nap, we got up and bathed all over in cold water and had a good stiff drink of brandy. For some time we examined each other's charms, toying and gloating until Ollie suddenly remembered my promise to let her taste the love-juice. I was nearly exhausted after a lickerish fondling of her handsome legs, big bottom and passionate looking titties, and I felt like another spend, but to make sure of a satisfactory charge I would always indulge in an act of exciting lewdness that would not only refill my reservoir, but give Ollie a new thrill.

Placing her on the edge of the bed, I told her to hold her legs apart with her knees up toward her face. This brought her salacious and luscious cunnie into full view and wide open. Getting some brandy, I held the puckering orifice open with my finger and thumb, then slowly poured in some brandy until the girl's vagina was full. I then held the lips together. Its fiery smart made her squeal and writhe. "Oh, Gott," she cried, "I'm on fire." I dropped to my knees and sucked all the liquor out of her pussy, and then proceeded to lap her off, which she enjoyed with lustful delight. I now had a handsome erection and sat on the bed telling Ollie to kneel on the floor between my legs. She was an apt pupil in sexual indulgences and quickly caught the meaning. She improved her opportunity to examine minutely every detail of my sexual splendors. I experienced a salacious thrill as the eager girl toyed and fingered my heavy, wrinkled balls and pulled back the tightly bound foreskin. She seemed to take playful delight in twisting the silky bunch of curls around her fingers with amorous kisses on the turgid knob and the light balls, which she tried to get into her mouth.

She prattled like a young girl over a doll: "Oh, what lufly big balls. They are full of juice I don't—wonder—darling—you—can shoot so —much—into—a girl," she ejaculated as she kissed the knob again and again, and slipping her moist, full lips around the spongy head, adjusted her mouth to it.

"Oh, Gee, Ollie," I exclaimed, "that's great. Hold it in your hand and move it up and down with sudden jerks—so—so—that's fine, girlie," I said as the skin yielded and I felt the friction on my rigid penis. The picture and thoughts of a voluptuously pretty girl performing the lascivious act of passionate love acted quickly on me. Ollie's eyes were turned up towards me, her buxom plump body clasped in my legs had started the sap of sexual love.

The girl felt it surging through my tight balls in her hand, "Oh, it's—coming—girlie—look and see it spurt." For a quick look she released the knob just as the cream sap was shooting out in the first spasm. Its pearly jet shot out thick and creamy. She gasped, then quickly clasped her pulpy red lips over the spouting knob and sucked ravenously as she squeezed the rigid shaft. The remainder of the splendid charge came in three long gushes, which filled her mouth. I howled with ecstasy. "Oh, girlie, that's so—good—suck—hard—jerk—fast—Oh, God!

that's gorgeous—OO—oo—Oh." I sank back, moaning and convulsed, as she continued to extract the last drops of aromatic liquor. She made a choking sound; "swallow it darling," I managed to mumble. I heard the gurgling sound as the impassive girl gulped down the hot juice. "Gee, Oh, my God, Ollie, what a peach of a cocksucker you are—that's great."

Ollie looked up into my face with eyes afloat and lips glistening with my pearly spend—"Oh, Goos, how nice it tastes. I luff it." She then gave a groan and sank to the floor, once more experiencing an orgasm induced by her lewd, and—to her—novel act. I had laid back on the bed, for the time being satiated and exhausted. Ollie crawled to my side and we both sank into a lustful sleep. It was nearly six when we awoke and dressed to prepare supper. The old folks returned at seven-thirty.

I was not very keen about lingering with the family, so I retired early to get back my normal sexual balance. It was three days later when I betook myself to the woods with my rifle to hunt, and was made the male actor in a comedy which was enacted in the following manner.

I realized that I had to conserve my powers to successfully enjoy the luxurious feasts of flesh coming my way. The daily mingling with two such sensuous, adorable females as Ollie and her mother titillated my lustful nature and kept me in a constant state of sexual excitement. Ollie had related her experiences to her mother, of the day alone with me, and she had, in turn, confessed to her husband how she had, in her starved condition, allowed the handsome boarder to give her a taste of real joy. He did not seem to be disturbed over his wife's indiscretions but was rather pleased to think that she could get relief. The idea filled him with lecherous delight to be once more able to perform the act himself, as we shall see in another chapter. Having learned from his wife what a wonderful penis I had, John was eager to see and made no bones about seeking the opportunity. It happened one morning when John took the fruit to me at the suggestion of his wife. He did not stop to knock but boldly walked in, finding me with my usual morning erection, inflamed and stately, expecting Nita for her morning piece.

John stood gasping with astonishment: "Gott," he exclaimed, "it's no wonder the Frau is crazy about you. Tell me, Mister Tolman, how can I get my old boy to stand like yours?" I was amused, then explained how, with certain treatment and lewd actions with his wife, he could have a respectable hardon. The vision of my magnificent tool and the prescribed treatment had an effect on the jaded passion of the man. I noticed the swelling in his tight breeches.

"Take it out, John, and let me see what you have got," I said. With a sudden pride, the man already feeling randy, displayed his penis, now showing signs of life. It was normal in size, but showed signs of atrophy.

"Ah, John," I said, "with a little coaxing you can have as big and stiff a penis as any woman would wish for. I'll go to town some day and get the very medicine to put life in that sleepy tool of yours." With a leer in his eyes and a groan, John cried out: "I could do it now." Just then Mrs. Nolsen came into the room. She wondered what had kept John so long, and so concluded to find out. When she saw her husband with his breeches open and his cock almost rigid, she gasped: "My boy," I said, "you two lie down here and have a good fuck." Nita needed no further urging.

John was quickly on top of her giving her a lively taste of his suddenly revived powers. The daughter, thinking it strange that both had remained upstairs so long ran up and into my room. The sight that met her astonished daze caused a scream: "Oh, how did it happen?" Then seeing me on my back and my penis standing straight up, she threw off her gown, jumped on me and quickly sheathed it in her pussy that was itching to be crammed. Delicious orgasms rewarded all four after a short orgy of fiery passion. Then I made known my plan for the rejuvenation of John, which was as follows:

My visit to the city resulted in purchasing a half dozen pairs of passionate silk stockings for each of the women. They were varied in color and delighted the girls who put them on and paraded up and down before us, showing off their pretty rounded voluptuously shaped legs. For John I bought an aphrodisiac in the shape of a dozen bottles of cantharides, and a specially made elastic binder and vibrator for use on his weak sexual organs. He was also presented with a book, *Rekindling Old Fires*. John was eager to begin the treatments.

It made Nita hot to think of the operations to come. The stage was set for that evening for the new, and to them, highly sensational operation of rejuvenating papa Nolsen,

Both women were to strip naked, but were to keep on a pair of red stockings, thus presenting an alluring picture of carnal lust. Both John and I stripped. John laid on the bed in front of a mirror. I directed Nita to get over him with her gorgeous bottom spread over his face and in a position to take his flabby penis in her mouth, which she did, rolling and winding her tongue about it. The act made her so randy that she spread her fat succulent pussy on John's face. Ollie giggled and John did not seem to like the idea of being smothered with a juicy cunt, but his tool began to stiffen.

Nita released it and it got soft again. I placed the elastic binder around the root close to his flabby testicles to hold in place the blood which would soon flow into his penis. I then directed Ollie to apply some cantharides to his knob and under it with a feather, and all down between his legs and over his balls. John began to twist and squirm from the effects of the blistering, teasing application. He began to howl and groan with the smart, but it was nevertheless effective. The atrophied parts got red and inflamed. His penis began to swell and stiffen slightly. Nita's eyes were popping as she gloated and gazed on the lewd performance. Both Nita and Ollie ran their hands down over his balls and penis, now splendidly stiff. "Oh, Gott! Oh, Gott!" cried Nita "At last! At last!" and throwing herself on the bed and spreading her magnificent thighs apart, cried out: "Coom, Coom, John, diddle me, foock me." He needed no second invitation for he was maddened with inflamed sexual desire and lustful emotions. Jumping onto his robust wife, he directed his inflamed and turgid tool and howled as he plunged it to the hilt into her hot cunnie. She screamed with joy. The scene of furious lust, when John indulged his rekindled passions, was a sight to behold. Nita spent again and again.

Ollie giggled and cried out: "Make it coom,

make it coom, papa, give her the juice, papa." John bellowed and shivered and groaned out his intense feelings of physical satisfaction when a long hot charge of sap gushed with spurts into the quivering womb of his wife, who crushed him between her buxom legs under the ecstatic agony of a complete orgasm. Her nipping cunnie extracted John's last drops of balsamic fluid amid cries and groans.

Ollie and I, infuriated with the voluptuous orgy got together on the same bed and assuaged our burning passions in a long drawn out feast of flesh.

We had many more days of the same kind of pleasures, after which it was time for me to return to my home in Washington.

Passing in and out of the house there, where I had a room, I frequently noticed a young lady of attractive face and figure with dark hair, who appealed to me very much.

At the very first I was not so much attracted to her until I noticed how she ogled me and the peculiar expression in her eyes whenever she looked my way. Then I began to get interested.

I began to study her. On closer observation I noticed that she was really quite pretty in a way, and that she possessed a tempting figure. One evening, as we were both returning to our respective rooms, I noticed her attire and discovered that she had the room next to mine, looking out onto a narrow balcony. She was attractively gowned in a light summer dress with short sleeves and the neck was cut low enough to reveal a plumpness of the bust. I tarried in the hall to let her precede me up the stairs.

Her rather short skirts displayed a pair of neat trim ankles and a pretty pair of shapely legs fitted in sheer smooth stockings. A pretty leg always made me long to see more, and I usually got a hunch as to whether or not I could feel of it. I managed to get a long look as she slowly preceded me up the stairs.

When we reached the top I spoke: "Pardon my intrusion and boldness but I would surely like to know the girl with such a pretty figure. You are most attractive."

She gasped and turned a frightened look toward me. I then got a good look at her face by means of the light overhead. I noted a peculiar, languorous look in her dark eyes. The face had all the marks of a nature which was more or less sensual.

I detected a look of lecherous longing as her eyes swept over me as if she were sizing me up. I made up my mind right then to get close to this beautiful girl. Her voice trembled and her bosom heaved with apparent emotion as she softly murmured: "I am Miss Taylor—who are you?" I introduced myself in my usual debonair manner, which seemed to attract her. "May I have the pleasure of calling on you?"

"Sometime," she bashfully answered as she passed through her door and closed it.

I noticed that she did not lock her door, having probably forgotten in her confusion. I entered my room and for the first time noticed the very thin partition between it and Miss Taylor's room. I later heard strange sounds like moans from a woman in distress. Then I distinctly heard a one-sided conversation; she was apparently talking to herself and this is what I heard: "Oh—Oh—if I could only have a lover like that man," she said trembling. "He—he—is so big and handsome."

I could hear her voice shake, as if she was under some great strain or emotion. I remembered the sensual expression on her face as the dreamy, pathetic eyes swept over me. Surely, I thought, the poor girl is in heat and apparently craves relief. While I was preparing for bed, and removing my shoes, my eye caught sight of a register in the partition, evidently used in the winter to allow a circulation of warm air. Upon examining it, I found that it opened very easily and through the grill frame I had a wide view of Miss Taylor's room. In my range of vision I saw the bed and an upholstered chair of generous capacity. Opposite this was a bureau with a large tilting mirror.

Miss Taylor was standing before the mirror, slowly removing her waist and gazing intently with that same languorous look at some pictures on the wall on either side of the mirror. Peering intently, I discovered that they were pictures of men, three of a stalwart pugilist in different poses stripped, but with a sash to hide his bulging genitals. Other pictures were of actors, presumably matinee idols, but the girl's eyes lingered on the muscular figure of the pugilist.

I saw her full red lips move as if she were talking to the fighter. Lifting up a pair of pretty white bubbies out of her corset, she bounced them up and down, then spoke in a low hysterical voice: "Oh, Jack, see my titties—come—to—me—and—fondle them."

I was no longer puzzled. The girl was hot and she was calling to Jack, the pugilist, as an imaginary lover. Her thoughts were lustily centered on the fleshy pleasures such a body would impart if she could but hold it in her arms and feel the strong sexual embrace and enjoyment that might result. In her impulsive emotions the girl tore off her corsets and then slipped out of her dress and drawers. She stood there revealed in nothing but her stockings and under-vest, which she quickly removed. When I saw what a finely built young girl she was, that settled it. She had to be gratified. I lay on my back so I could better contemplate with ease what might transpire in the girl's room.

She was about twenty and I could plainly see her white nude body, rich in lovely contours and graceful curves, together with a very disturbing view of her dark thickly haired pussy and her white cherry tipped bubbies. They made me rampant, and my tool was standing straight up. I doubtless would have made a rush through the door to the girl if my curiosity had not gotten the better of me. I gasped when I saw her press her hand to her pussy and insert a finger and again gaze at the picture of the pugilist as she vigorously rubbed and worked her finger in and out.

Her feelings were getting the better of her and as she worked herself up to a pitch of passionate frenzy, a wave of erotic emotion spread a lovely glow over her shapely charms. As if suddenly thinking of something, she unlocked the bureau drawers and extracted a book and a small packet from which she selected several pictures, evidently an obscene book, as I later discovered.

Reclining on the edge of the bed, with one leg hanging over the side, she switched on a reading lamp over her head, which gave me a brilliantly lighted view of the girl's tempting and sensual body in a voluptuous pose. The line of my vision took in every detail of a plump and well defined cunnie between a pair of lovely white thighs. The contrast of the dark thick curls made her belly and thighs appear like alabaster.

Adjusting her pillow, the girl began reading, holding two of the pictures on the edge of the book, leaving her right hand free. Occasionally she would gloat on her own charms reflected in the tilting mirror. At the same time she would pinch and titillate the stiff red nipples of her firm round bubbies.

The swelling, curly mound and pretty round belly began to rise and fall with convulsions and erotic longings as she gloated over the book and pictures. Inflamed to a frenzy the girl's hand slipped down and covered the restless pussy. Then with her middle finger she sought to appease her passions with a rapid nervous thrust and pressure on the burning clitty. Suddenly, apparently coming to a passage in her book which inflamed the poor girl, she gasped aloud. I heard a smothered cry—Oh, how lovely—how I'd—like—to—be—in her place." Then holding the pictures close she gazed with languorous eyes and clasped the whole of the plump curly cunnie in her hand with two fingers in it, squeezing it hard.

The heavy breathing and groans told me of her approaching crisis. Dropping the pictures, her head went back to the pillows. Her limbs twitched and quivered. The pretty bubbies trembled. Then with a convulsive heave and choking expressions of pleasure, as "—Oh—Oh—how—good," spasm after spasm of voluptuous ecstasy swept over her in a thrilling orgasm.

She trembled and shivered terrifically, holding her hand very tightly over her cunnie for a short while, and then seemed to die away in a languorous doze for a few minutes. When she finally picked up her book and continued to read she was so worked up that she was as frantic for relief as before. All the time she had held her hand on her moist cunnie, though without moving it at all. Occasionally she would pick up the pictures again and look at them and then go back to her book. This she kept up for some little time, for the book was apparently very interesting.

Finally, however, she threw down the book and began irritating herself in real earnest. Her magnificent bubbies she could just pull up so as to make her lips grasp the nipples and these she sucked hard, at the same time playing her fingers around her cunnie. Then she used one hand to inflame her clitoris and with the other hand she inserted a finger deep in her cunnie until, judging by her emotions, she was coming, she frantically drove three fingers deep into it and worked them in and out fast until she died away in a glorious spend.

This sight was too much for me. I was lying on my back and was naked. I had become so inflamed and highly sensitized that the scene was like a match to dry powder. My erect and well primed penis went off and shot stretches of pearly juice high into the air. It was all that I could do to withhold a cry of delight, for the spend and the sensations accompanying it were terrific. It fell in little puddles all over my belly as I watched the throes and last tremors of the gratified girl. She got up, put on her nightgown and replacing the book and pictures in the bureau drawer, retired.

I quietly closed the register and crawled into

bed. In the morning I awoke with my usual morning hardon and lay awake planning how to have Miss Taylor and to get a glimpse of her book and pictures. I heard her go out at seven-thirty. Getting up and dressing I took the key to my bureau drawer, feeling sure that it would also fit her drawer. Going to her door I found it unlocked. Entering and closing the door I tried the key. It fitted. I found the book that the girl had been reading and the package of pictures. The book was called *The Education of Laura* and was intended to inflame passion and instruct girls in sexual pleasures. The photos were faithful pictures of men and women together in all the known positions of indulgence.

No wonder I thought that she was a masturbator. But why she resorted to it was a mystery to me for she was a girl to attract any man sexually. I made my plans to see her that evening when she would return from work. She returned and dressed for dinner in a most attractive dress, and for some unknown reason left off her corsets and put on a pair of those late fashionable hosettes coming just above the calf, leaving the knees bare.

Apparently she was prone to making herself attractive to men. On this occasion she wore very little under a thin organdy dress, through which could be seen the distinct outlines of a remarkably well-shaped leg and thigh. She also left off her drawers. It might have been that she wanted to make a hit with me, but that I didn't know yet. She was standing in the main hall before the open front door when I came out of the dining room. My alert eye caught the alluring view as the light showed through the girl's skirts, outlining the attractive curves and contours.

Passing out on the large veranda, where there were chairs, all occupied but one, which Miss Taylor took, I seated myself on a step below and facing her. Glancing up I had a tantalizing view of the bare knees, which were crossed in careless girlish pose. Several times I caught glimpses of a dark brown tuft between the plump white thighs. I was getting too conspicuously uncomfortable and randy for comfort. Miss Taylor noticed the restless shifting and gloating eyes as I glanced up. She too, got restless. The fact that I was watching her with lustful longing aroused all the sensual fires in her passionate body. Did I really like her, was probably the girl's thought as she watched me out of half-closed eyes. Strategy was one of my strong assets. Suddenly I arose and asked her to take a stroll to get an ice-cream soda. At first she demurred, then bashfully consented. Once out on the street she became a little more sociable.

"If you don't mind, Mister Tolman, I'd like to have a gingerale highball," she said as we walked along.

"Sure thing, my dear," I answered, "sodas are not much good when one is as uncomfortable as we are. By the way what is your first name?"

"Margery—Madge for short," replied the girl. For an hour she conversed and showed absolutely no signs of the seething desires that were teasing her young pussy. Her nature was not revealed. On the way home I took her arm, delicately passing my hand up and down the soft cool flesh.

"Madge, dear," I said to her in my tenderest way, "mayn't I sit with you in your room tonight? I have something most important to tell you."

The poor girl got so frightened and flushed she almost collapsed, but answered in a low trembling tone: "I—I don't know—would—would it be safe?"

"Why, my dear girl, I hope you are not afraid of me, and no one would know anything about it in your room," I said reassuringly. She said nothing but I could detect a tumultuous storm in the heaving of her firm round bubbies and trembling steps. Reaching the house I begged her to remain on the steps until I got to my room, then when hearing her enter her room, I would call. She followed the instructions to the letter.

I knocked on the door. I then heard a fluttering voice: "C—Come in." When I stood before her in a white silk shirt turned down at the neck and short sleeves and wearing blue flannel trousers that displayed my muscular limbs, Margery gasped and almost fainted, but finally said:

"Oh, Mister Tolman, I have never allowed a man in my room before. Tell me what you want with a poor working girl like me? You are so big and handsome that you embarrass me."

The door was closed and covered with drapery that smothered out all sounds of voices from within. Madge remained standing as I stepped up to her side, and anxious of my opportunity to begin, I said:

"My dear little girl, what I am going to say is for your own good and safety." She again got frightened, her eyes usually so languorous and wide, her scarlet lips hung apart as she breathlessly waited.

"My dear Madge," I said tenderly, "do you know that you are doing yourself an awful injury and injustice every time you indulge your passions as you did last night?"

The frightened and surprised girl gasped, "My God!" and then fainted. I caught her in my arms and picking her up, I sat down in a large easy chair and held the unconscious girl on my lap. The feeling of her soft corsetless body and pressure of the soft round bottom on my penis inflamed me instantly.

My tool stiffened and assumed its splendid throbbing proportions. Reaching a bottle of smelling salts I saw on the bureau, I held it to her nose, then chaffed her hands. Pulling up her skirts I slapped and squeezed the plump dimpled knees. My other hand was molding a lovely tittie. My lips were grazing a velvety cheek. Presently Madge showed signs of reviving. I fondled her bare knees with affectionate caresses and pressures on the nerves that I knew would excite sensations of passion, moving my hand always further up. Her flesh was like the softest velvet.

My rampant tool was moving and bounding against her little pussy. Of course she could feel it through her clothing. Her eyes opened, she drew a long breath and cuddled closer to me, then in a frightened voice she asked:

"Where am I? What has happened?"

"In your lover's arms, who thinks you are the most beautiful and sweetest little peach in the world. Kiss me, Madge," I said. She didn't speak, but I could tell that she was gradually warming up from her restless breathing and squirming bottom, but she did not want me to know it. She was shy and somewhat frightened at the suddenness of the situation. Finally when she remembered what I had told her of the night before, she straightened out and putting on an air of injury from the liberty and accusation, she stimulated a resentment, but she knew that she was guilty.

"How do you know—how can you—say—such a thing? How dare you?" I was amused. "Why my dear," I replied, "it was very easy. I was in my room and I overheard your moans and cries. I was alarmed and seeing that register I took a chance of looking through it to ascertain the trouble, and what I saw you doing to yourself made me feel terrible to think that a lovely young girl like you would injure yourself in that way. Tell me Margery, why do you do it, when you can have a lover?"

"Then with a trembling voice and tears in her dark eyes, she related how she had been taught to gratify her passions, that all her life she had been a victim of uncontrollable passions—that because a girl friend had once let a man have her and she became pregnant and she was always afraid to let a man have her out of fear.

"Why, Gus, that same girl always after that gratified herself with her fingers. She was like me, always hot, and it was she who taught me to do it to myself, giving me naughty books and pictures, she got from a man. Is it any wonder that I do it?"

"Not a bit," I answered. "But don't you know that you could have a man without serious results?"

"No! How?" cried the girl. I then explained if a girl indulged her passions with a man in the week before her periods or used a strong solution for a douche before and after each time, she would be perfectly safe.

The effect of my hand on her knees and my throbbing tool had so inflamed Madge she was in a tumultuous flutter. "OO—oo, Gus," she gasped. "I must tell my friend Trixie." Then winding her arms about me she kissed me with her moist red lips, clinging to me with ardent longing. Suddenly and with impulsive emotion, Madge parted her thighs and whispered:

"Fondle me—Gus—I—I'm—I'm so passionate." I laid my hand over the curly plump nest. "Oh, Gus—put your finger into it—and make me—spend."

"Ah, no, my dear," I said. "I'm going to break you of that habit, it's not good nor healthy for you and besides it's not nautral. Why can't we have the real pleasures together? It's so much lovelier."

"Oh, Gus, I'd like to, but I'm afraid. I'd surely get caught and I've never done that in my life. I haven't even seen a real live thing, only the pictures that I have."

"Well, my dear girl," I said, "do you want to see one and even have it in you and make you feel so good—oh so good, better than you have ever felt when you did it with your finger?"

"Oh, heavens, yes, I'm just insane for it, but I'm too scared of it."

I had been fondling her smooth round belly and tickling her highly sensitive clitty. I stopped and asked her to let me stand up and show her something that beat a finger or candle all to bits. Curious and eager with passion to see what she had seen in hot lascivious dreams, the girl stood leaning against a long library table as

I lowered my trousers and released my prodigious tool. It popped out and stood proudly erect and flaming with fiery vigor.

The girl, with eyes aflame with wonder and interest, just stood and gazed. Her face was a study, first blushing a deep scarlet, then distorted with fear, her face lighting up with a hungry gleam of lustful passion. With a choking gulp Madge managed to speak in a half whisper:

"Heavens, Gus, it doesn't look anything like those in my pictures, but it's glorious—a monster. My God! How can a girl take it? I never saw a real live one before."

I moved towards the girl and she almost shrank. "Feel it, girlie," I said. It won't hurt you." Slyly and with girlish modesty Madge placed her hand on it, her fingers just encircling it. They slipped along until her hand held the turgid purple knob in its palm, she squeezed it, then gasped, her panting bubbies heaving and rising and falling in a tumult of erotic sensations.

Remembering some of the lewd acts shown in the photos and described in her book, Madge became very eager.

"May I kiss it, Gus?" she asked. "Why, of course, if you'll let me kiss yours," I replied.

"Oh—where? when? how?"

I quickly cleared the table and placed some cushions upon it.

"Now I'll show you for you are a real scout, Madge, and one of the most lovable and fuckable girls I ever knew," I said. I picked her up and placed her on the table with her peachy bottom on the edge, and directed her to place her feet on the back of a chair I had drawn up behind me. It was my usual preliminary to this, my favorite position to win a woman over. Throwing her dress back and exposing Madge's delectable charms, I feasted my eyes on one of the prettiest bellies and pussies I had ever seen. Such lovely legs and thighs, such a plump and creamy bottom, spread out under the fluffy bunch of dark brown curls, through which the pulpy lips of her moist cunnie were pouting, opening and closing with hot longing.

A bright red clitty protruded stiff and pert. Altogether, Margery's pussy offered about as tempting a feast as any man would wish to see between a pair of shapely legs. I patted and caressed the round white belly and velvety plump inside of the girl's thighs, all the time gloating on the delicious morsel nestled in a thick tuft of silky curls, till I was hungry for it. "Oh, Gus," she said, "will you do what the book calls—lapping the cunt?"

"Why, of course, Madge, and a lot more," I replied as I proceeded to lay back the thick soft lips and opened up the red meaty interior, disclosing a small puckering orifice, with palpitant longing. I placed my mouth to the distended gap and the fragrant mellow lips closed about my mouth. At the first thrust of my tongue, Margery almost screamed from the new and novel sensation. The faster my tongue glided in and out, the tighter she clasped my head between her convulsed thighs. All she could utter was a trembling. "Oh, how good—that—feels—Oh, God, don't stop!"

I then began a lively tongue play on the stiff clitoris till the poor girl was almost insane with a desire to spend. "For heaven's sake, bring it," she pleaded pathetically.

"Yes, pet, I'll make you go off and spend more than you ever did before. When did you say you were last unwell?"

"Ten days ago," replied Margery with quickened delight. "Good," I said, getting to my feet. I had placed the table in front of the mirror and I tilted it to reflect every detail. Taking a soft shapely leg under each arm, I opened Margery's moist and quivering cunnie and guiding my restless penis, I rubbed the purple knob all about the gap.

"Watch in the glass," I said, as I titillated the sensitive clitoris. The girl was watching every detail, her eyes limpidly languorous, her crimson lips parted in a sensuous smile. When I began to force the head of the ferocious tool into the tight puckering orifice she gave a smothered groan: "You'll never get that big thing into me. It'll kill me."

"Yes, dear, it'll kill you with pleasure." I got the head well in and then stopped to play with the creamy bubbies and tickle her clitty and wait for her to get accustomed to the stretched feeling. She began to sigh and squirm and then murmured softly: "Oh, Gus, it feels so good—I—I—think that you can go a little farther." She closed her eyes and then gripped the table when I made a lunge that sent the turgid tool into the juicy depths till it bumped against her womb. She gave a smothered scream, her eyes were swimming and her bubbies heaving with a voluptuous sensation. Slowly and sensuously I moved back and forth now.

"There, Madge," I said softly, "isn't that nicer than your finger or a candle?"

"Oh, God, yes," she exclaimed, it's heavenly. Do it faster." I held her belly and with lively hip action, I twisted and screwed the lustful creature. "OO—Oh, it's—lovely—Oh—I'm dying—hold— me— it's— com—ing— Oh—how—good—now—now—Oh, darling." I distinctly felt her throbbing womb as each spasm of her orgasm shook her inflamed body and made her breathe hard and stammer her expressions of voluptuous sensations. The amorous girl was so inflamed that her unappeased passion made her call out in her agony of erotic emotions, "Don't stop, for God's sake, don't stop—I'm not half gratified—I never imagined—it—was half so—lovely to be properly fucked."

Suddenly realizing my immense tool was still stiff and in full vigor and believing that I had spent, Margery looked at me with amazement and dreamy eyes and said, "Didn't you come?" "No, my lovely little Madge, "I'll not spend until I've made you go off again, and say—no more finger fucks for me."

"I'll never do it that way after this," she replied. "I shall tell my friend all about it. Will you give her a treat like this some time, too?"

"Sure," I replied, "if she'd like me well enough to let me." And then I continued to feast my fleshy appetite on the girl's lascivious charms. Margery indulged her own sensual nature and revelled in thoughts of lascivious pleasures in company with me and her friend Tessie. "Oh, she will, Tess will go wild when she meets you and sees your lovely big thing," she said. "She is just crazy to have a big strong man. Can't we three make a party some night together?"

"Of course. We'll go to a hotel," I answered, pleased.

"Oh, Gus, you make me so passionate, I could scream. Do it faster!"

I pressed the turgid bursting head against her womb and made it throb and tickle her, sending thrills of lustful emotions over her trembling body. "Oh, Gus! Oh!" she moaned, as I worked my tool in and out with a lustful spiral motion.

"How's that, girlie?" I asked.

"Oh, it's great—it's—com—ing—fuck me—fuck me hard—Oh, my God!" And her eyes rolled and sank back into her head, showing only the whites.

I groaned. I had held back as long as I could. "Oh, baby," I hollered. "I'm coming, too—suck it—so—so—" I cried, as Margery's nipping cunnie closed with convulsive spasms. "Ah,—there—there," as I shot a charge of hot balsamic juice into the girl's belly. She lay still and received the balmy delirious juice in ecstasy.

Before the last sensuous thrill passed, I picked up the half-conscious girl and carried her to the bed with my reeking stiff still in her. Getting off my shirt, I managed to divest Margery of her clothes and then we lay for some time in a languid sea of blissful content, till I got eager for another orgasm.

Getting on top of her, I placed it in her with frenzied frictional thrusts till we both died away again in a voluptuously complete finish. I got up and returned to my room to let the poor girl sleep off the effects of our dream of pleasures such as she had never experienced before.

Two days later I met Madge and she passed the word to me: "Tessie will be here to meet you at eight o'clock in my room. Come at that time and knock."

I made a careful preparation for conquest and a night with my latest finds. First engaging a room at a hotel of unquestioned privacy and then completing a toilet that would prove the way to conquest. I wore a Palm Beach suit over a sheer silk shirt with no underwear. I had, without a doubt, an attractive figure and my close-fitting trousers displayed my muscular limbs and abnormal sexual development to good advantage.

Promptly at eight o'clock I heard Madge in her room, and then a cheery voice: "Gee, Madge, I'm just wild to meet your friend. How do I look?" asked Tessie as she threw off her cape. "Say, Tess," said Madge, "he will go wild and eat you alive when he sees your bare back, it's lovely." She had left her entire back exposed to her waistline with but a narrow line over each shoulder, the front being so thin that even the stiff red nipple points of a pair of the prettiest bubbies stuck out alluringly. Tessie was taller than Madge, with remarkably pretty arms and legs—not large but tempting in form and shape. She possessed a bottom that was ravishing in contour and agility. She wore nothing else but a lace petticoat and black silk stockings, gartered well above the knees.

When I answered the call to enter, the vision that met my gaze, startled me. "Miss Tessie Bangs," said Margery, introducing us, "this is Mr. Tolman." I bowed low as I took Tessie's hand and kissed it. She shivered for she felt a thrill go through her. "Surely," I said, "this is a refreshing pleasure." Tess was speechless as her eyes swept over my figure and when she could speak, her voice was low and musical, "I am equally delighted," she said, "I do hope your pleasure will be equal to mine."

"Well," I said, "judging from appearance, when I see more of you, I know that my pleasure will know no bounds. You are the peachiest looking and most delectable looking chicken I've met in years." She resented the term I gave her. Her big blue eyes flashed and with a vivacious but injured dignity she retorted: "I beg your pardon Mister Tolman, I'm no chicken and you needn't think that because Margery Taylor fell for you and you happen to be a handsome brute, I shall fall, too."

I saw that she meant every word and that I would be obliged to trim her claws as I had often done before with others. I replied, looking steadily and smilingly into her flashing eyes, "You are a chicken and a deucedly tempting bird to broil, and with proper seasoning you will make fine eating." Tessie gasped, for she well knew what I meant.

"I never met up with such nerve before," she said. Her practiced eye caught sight of the bulging outlines of my abnormal sexual charm, already showing signs of vigor and life. She jumped back with a twist of her pretty shoulders and shaking my pendulous bubbies. "My, God, man, but you are immense," still gloating on my tool and balls, which showed plainly through my light trousers.

"Pshaw, Tess," spoke up Margery, "you ought to see it out and stiff. Take it out, Gus." It was my plan to work Tess up until she was at the point of begging for it, but as she seemed curious and willing, I unbuttoned my trousers, but first I stepped up to her and without warning clasped her lithe and willowy form in my arms and pressed her mound to my rapidly stiffening tool by placing a convulsive hand on her plump bottom.

She tried to wriggle loose, but the more she wriggled the stiffer my penis became till it throbbed against her pussy. The sensation was so exciting to her that she just hung limp in my arms and shivered. I kissed her and then when my mouth closed over her ruby lips, I thrust my tongue into her mouth and squeezed her soft bottom with both my eager hands.

She returned my kisses almost unconsciously as she gazed at me with limpid, langurous eyes. Once or twice she half clung to me and when I began to run my tongue between her lips, it was too much for her. She just hung onto me enough to keep from falling.

All of a sudden, tearing her mouth loose, she cried out in a frantic appeal:

"Stop, I don't mean to let you get fresh with me!"

My hands and touchings were doing their work, however. I slipped one hand all over her smooth bare back, tickling her spine at the same time and running my tongue around her neck under her chin and ears. Her eyes flushed, her bottom wriggled—she laughed and then began to scratch. I realized I had an unusually spiteful chicken to deal with. Shaking my trousers loose, my rampant penis came forth in all its passionate splendor.

"Oh, look Tessie," said Margery, laughing. In her excitement and struggle one of her hands came in contact with it. Like oil on troubled waters, her flush of injured dignity subsided and she melted in my arms like jelly in a mold, and hung limp from surprise and suddenly aroused emotions. At first she couldn't speak, she seemed so dazed. Then with sudden curiosity, her hand went to the prodigious, throbbing weapon, her long tapering fingers closing about it. Gasping she drew back to look: "Good God," she exclaimed, "what is it, a bone or a club?"

"The stick that you are going to be broiled on, my dear," I said.

"Never, never!" cried the astonished girl, looking at it and squeezing the long hard shaft. "Why that thing would kill me."

"Aw, go on," laughed Margery.

"I'll be," said Tess to her, "you never had that brute of a thing in you. You told a fib. I never heard of a man having a tool like that."

"Ah, Tess, just you wait until it's in you, and you'll see all the stars in creation and go off like you never did before, and I'll bet that you'll never want anything else. Why Tess, it beats a finger or a candle a thousand ways. To be broiled on that darling cock is a treat you'll never forget."

Then turning to me, Margery kissed me and said: "Strip, Gus, and let Tessie see." "I will if she'll do the same," I replied. Margery led the way and began to undress. She hadn't much on to be taken off. Tessie was now gay and festive, lively as could be. She and Margery were soon stripped to their stockings and I gazed with lustful enthusiasm on two of the most charming and fuckable damsels I ever laid my eyes on. Tessie was perfect in symmetry and shapeliness. Tall and graceful, she was exquisitely rounded with a pair of luscious, slightly drooping bubbies, not as large as Margery's but just as lovely to play with and mold in the hands. She had a prominent, protruding mound covered with a profusion of thick blonde curly hair like silk, through which the pretty deep slit of a plump pussy could be seen.

I was now more than rampant to get at it. I stripped naked, to my socks. When Tessie's eyes swept over me, she gasped with carnal admiration, her eyes almost popping out of her head as she gloated on my penis, which she expected to be broiled upon.

"My God, Madge," she exclaimed, "I don't wonder that you fell for him, he is magnificent, but I'll have to see you take that tool before I'll believe you had it in your little cunnie," she said, as she again felt of it with trembling hands, trying to pull it away from my belly, where it stood stiff as a bar of iron. It slipped from her hand and sprung back with a thud. Tessie giggled and continued to enjoy the unusual vigorous elasticity of the perky, obstreperous penis.

"Let's get busy," I said. "I'm getting too hot for comfort and I'm anxious for a drink. We'll have a round, go out for a highball, and then go to a room I've engaged for the night. You two lovely chickens have to broil on both sides thoroughly, so let's get busy while the bone is in good form.

"I want to see Madge take it first," said Tessie with a mischievous and lustful thrust of her naughty handsome bottom. I arranged the table with cushions and directed Margery to lie on it as on the first night when she was initiated.

Margery looked most tempting and desirable as she lay with her legs wide open and her peachy, salacious pussy ready for the stick. Two firm milky bubbies, with their stiff red nipples pointing straight up and out, invited kisses.

"Now, Gus," laughed Tessie, "do exactly what you did to her the other night. I want to see how you got that awful thing into her tight little cunnie."

I seated myself directly in front of the voluptuous little pussy with Margery resting her pretty fat legs on each shoulder. "My God," exclaimed Tessie, all curious and getting hotter every minute, "I've had some fun in my life, but I was never kissed there."

I began my feast with hot kisses on the pretty rounded belly and on the soft white insides of her thighs to arouse keener sensations of desire. I then titillated her with lively tongue play on her perky, red clitoris.

Madge began to moan, but when the ardent sweep of my tongue along the pouting slit penetrated the puckering orifice, she trembled and cried out: "Oh—Tess—ie—wait—till he does this to you—Oh, it's so good—Oh." When I thrust my tongue into the salacious meaty depths of her pussy and tickled her womb, Margery suppressed a scream, shook all over and cried: "Oh, Tessie—suck my titties, quick—I'm—I'm—com—com—ing." Tessie quickly took a big red nipple in her mouth and tickled the other one with her fingernails. As nothing excites a woman to spend as quickly as that, Margery just moaned and heaved and clutched at her friend and cried out: "Oh, Tess! There—

there—Oh—how good—OO—oo—Oh!"

I received her sweet, creamy spend on my tongue and sucked it up as it flowed freely. She being thoroughly lubricated, I got to my feet, then taking the bursting red tool in my hand I worked the swollen inflamed head all about in the juicy slit, while Tessie stood by holding apart the fat lips and watching the all-absorbing and lascivious act of broiling Madge. Her eyes wide, almost popping out, her snowy bosom heaving with excitement and her pussy itching and twitching, Tessie saw me plunge my frenzied penis into Margery to the hilt. Madge stuffed her fist into her mouth to smother her cries and screams of lustful pleasure. I worked my tool back and forth with sensuous effect and Tessie, watching it as it went in and out, almost screamed herself.

"Hurry, Madge, I'm just dying for a piece," Tessie again tickled the quivering red nipples. Madge cried out: "Oh, God! It's coming—what a lovely—fuck." Her voice died away. I pulled out my inflamed tool reeking with her pearly spend and lifting Madge up I laid her on the bed, telling Tessie to get on the table. I had not spent for I wanted to save it for the excited Tessie.

The table was before the mirror and when Tessie discovered that she could watch herself being fucked, she laughed in glee. I stood for a moment to gloat on the exquisitely lovely charms of this delectable girl, fondling every part of her. Then taking my place again in the chair between the prettily shaped legs outstretched for the kisses, I gazed lustfully at one of the prettiest and alluring pussies I ever saw. Profusely covered with silky blonde hair, it stood out plump and impudent. Tessie had what might be termed a real hardon, for the outer lips were hard and horny and her clitty stuck out its red nose stiffly. I noted the delectable, sweet scented, savory condition of her private parts. Holding the soft cheeks of her fat bottom apart, I gazed fondly at all her beauties when she anxiously wound her fat legs around my neck and exclaimed, "My God, what a lover you are!"

I now buried my nose in her slit and worked my tongue deep in. She bit her lips and exclaimed with a deep moan: "Suck me."

I then gave her the same tonguing I had just given Madge, but I fairly ate the mellow meaty interior with lively tongue thrusts.

I gathered all the ripe parts on her cunnie into my mouth and sucked like mad, with my tongue rubbing her stiffened clitty. Tessie was trembling and quivering all over. "Wow! Oh! Ouch!" she cried. Her cry aroused Margery from her languor, and she came smiling to the side of the table.

"Oh, Madge," she cried, "he's sucking the life out of me—oo—oo—Oh, how I'm spending!"

"Isn't it great?" asked Madge, patting Tessie's titties and pinching the little stiff nipples.

"Oh, it's heavenly," replied Tessie as she died away in another swoon of voluptuous ecstasy. I jumped up then with a terrible hardon that was actually painful. It was forbidding in appearance. Tessie had never seen nor dreamed of a penis like it before. Handsome it was, to say the least, with its splendid appendages like ripe fruit bursting with a wealth of rich juices.

Tessie's eyes, languorous with the sensual after effects of a copious spend, looked with fear as I stood beside her. In a voice trembling with apprehension, she said: "Let—let me feel it, Gus, it's awful."

I stepped closer to her, and she felt the awful thing from the balls to the tip of the turgid knob as if testing and measuring its size and power. I took it in my hand and moved the knob around in her neck, under her chin and ears. She murmured:

"Oh, you beauty. Now I'm ready—Oh, Gus, be careful, won't you?"

"Yes," I answered.

"Then broil me and do it good, I'm hot as a blister," and to Madge she said, "don't leave me, Madge, and give me a handkerchief."

I took a pretty leg under each arm and Madge stood by to assist. She pulled the inflamed fat lips apart, revealing its red meaty interior and puckering orifice from which oozed traces of her recent spending. I moved my tool up and down and rubbed the quivering inflamed clitty. "Oh, God! that's exciting," she cried out suddenly, "put it in quick."

I placed the almost bursting knob at the entrance and pushed. She gasped and stuffed the handkerchief into her mouth to smother a cry of pain. With the head just inside, I waited for her to get accustomed to the stretching. The nipping stricture was maddening to me. Tessie relieved her mouth long enough to say, "All of it, Gus—I—I—want it all!" Replacing the wad of handkerchief in her mouth, she grabbed Margery. I braced myself and clutching the girl's squirming hips, I crammed my penis into the tight hot depths till it was completely sheathed.

How she did squirm and writhe. I hollered myself with sensuous delight, exclaiming:

"Oh, Tes—sie—what a perfect cunt you have."

Her pain had subsided, she removed the cloth from her mouth, her crimson lips parted in a smile of joy. Margery bit and sucked the stiff red nipples whilst I tickled her navel. "What a pretty belly. What pretty legs. You two girls are the peachiest chickens to fuck that I ever knew," I whispered as I moved my straining spear out and in, producing a fury of erotic thrills in us both. Tessie could not prolong the delightful indulgence long enough.

"Gee," she gasped, "I wish that it could last all night."

Once her tongue was loosened she became obscene as her erotism increased. I was getting a royal feast of voluptuous sensation. The climax was approaching us both. Tessie's curly blonde head rolled from side to side—she clawed at her stomach and her milky panting bubbies as they rose and fell faster and faster with her quickened breath. I put my most masterful strokes to the frenzied girl with agonizing thrills.

She hollered in smothered gusts, "Oh, God! I'm coming!" Her arms dropped to her side.

"Somebody kiss me! Hold me! I'm dying! Oh —oo—oo." Margery giggled. I grabbed the exploding girl in my arms, crushed a soft tittie in each hand and smothered her gasping cries with a tonguing kiss. She sucked the tongue almost out of me.

"There, you hot little cunt, take my sap, it's —good for you," I said as I poured hot streams of delicious juice into the trembling girl, the jets piercing her like needles and bringing a secondary spend in which Tessie's eyes rolled in erotic delirium. I laid her gently back and completed my own double spend in a blinding orgasm which shook me to my toes.

"Heavens," cried Margery, "you've got me so hot I can scarcely wait for another piece." Tessie wriggled off the table and staggered as if drunk to the bed, where she laid in a half-faint from the effect of the frenzied orgy.

I quickly got a bottle of brandy. We all had a stiff drink and prepared to go out. After Tessie had had two drinks she was as lively as a cricket and ready for a frolic. Like a contortionist she writhed and displayed her enticing charms to excite the lewdest passions. Her sensual nature was thoroughly fired after getting a generous taste of my powers and my skillfully manipulated tool. She was wanton to the core. Before I had completed my toilet, Tessie kissed my penis. Being now soft and normal she drew it into her mouth and cuddled it with her tongue. "Gee," she exclaimed, "I'd like to suck you off." We were all hotter than blisters and ready for anything. We left the house unseen and were soon in the room I had engaged for the night. I ordered highballs with plenty of ginger. Both girls stripped, and jumping onto the table, they did a most exciting and lewd dance. Tessie was more agile than Madge, but Madge's movements were far more suggestive and voluptuous.

They had often practiced together when under the influence of lecherous desire to indulge their wanton passion and to induce a spend would press their pussies together and rub and twist with their titties crushed together till a frenzied orgasm would reward their efforts. I watched the lascivious performance till I was so hot my turgid gun was standing cocky and purple and almost ready to go off. I grabbed both girls and fell with them on the bed. I was about to mount Tessie, when she cried out:

"Hold on Gus. I'm hot, too hot for an old-fashioned fuck. I want a hoochie cootchie diddle."

"How's that?" I asked.

She then directed me to lie across two chairs with my head on the bed and my knees hanging over the edge of the farthest chair while Madge was to straddle my head and press her cunnie to my mouth. This was a new trick but I liked the idea and at once arranged for it. I first drew both girls to the edge of the bed, with their plump bottoms on the edge, with their legs wide apart and knees drawn up.

The quivering swollen cunnies were then gaping open, the orifice of each pouting for something stiff. I took a highball, and holding Madge's little hole well open, I poured into it a goodly portion and then held the lips together so it wouldn't spill, to let it soak in and heat up the tight little box. Dropping to my knees, I deftly placed my mouth to the lips and sucked out the warmed up liquor. She screamed and wriggled her fat bottom. She was consumed with longing. I gave Tessie the same treat and when I had sucked out the last drops she writhed and screamed.

"My God, that was brutal. I was hot enough without that. Hurry up and get on the chairs and I'll screw the balls off you while you lap Madge." I got awful randy as Tessie took her position while I lay as she directed, with my erect penis standing straight and rigid, ready to burst. Tessie cuddled it in her soft bubbies and kissed it again with thrusts of her tongue in the little orifice.

Our passions spent, we fell back on the bed. I was asleep as was Tessie. Madge, in her state of erotic feelings, began working her fingers in her moist slit, but was so passionate and eager for another piece, she knew that she had first to get it stiff. Following descriptions she had read, of a way to get a man's penis to stand, Madge hung over me and lifted my seemingly dead penis into her mouth with her tongue after tickling the wrinkled balls. When she got half of the soft mass into her mouth she slipped her tongue around and around the head as she gently chewed the soft root. I stirred, woke up and not thinking which of my partners was at me, clutched Tessie and kissed her, feeling and molding her titties, now firm after a rest. She, too, awoke.

"Oh, Gus, do you want me again so soon?" I then perceived that it was Madge who was eating it up.

"Look Tess," I said. "Madge wants it. Poor girl, she's hungry." When Tessie saw Madge frantically chewing the mouthful, she rolled the splendid reservoir of sap in her one hand. "That's right, Madge," she said. "That'll make it come up if you want a piece. I'm ready for one myself." Tess tickled me, sucked my hard nipples and between the two amorous girls, I began to get stiff. My penis got too big for Madge's mouth. Letting it languidly out, she said:

"I do want a piece. I'm hot from my toes to my hair."

I handled both quivering cunnies, sticking a finger into each. This would always make me hot. My tool swelled and stiffened to grand proportions till I had one of my characteristic morning hardons.

"Give it to Madge first," cried Tess. "She found it first." I got on top of the plump, passionate girl and gave her the liveliest, hottest fuck I ever put to a girl, till she groaned and screamed in an ecstatic satisfying orgasm. I finished her off and left my rigid tool in her till she swooned off in a sensuous die-away, having restrained my own desire to spend.

I preferred my morning feast between Tessie's soft, shapely legs in her tight excitable little box. I wanted to feel Tessie's long lithe limbs wind about me and once more experience the ecstatic spend by her wriggling bottom and toe-curling, sucking cunnie.

"Heavens, you're bigger than ever," she exclaimed. "It's just grand. Oh, Gee, how lovely, umm." She groaned with each straining thrust and throb. Tessie twined her pretty legs around me and thus braced, she not only met my thrusts with effective bucking up motions but could wriggle and twist with a screwing motion that thrilled me with lustful zeal.

Her cries and shuddering frame told of the delightful spends she was having. When I could no longer restrain myself to prolong the voluptuous feast, I gathered the trembling plump form of Tessie in my arms and gazing down in her misty rolling eyes, groaned out:

"Oh, Tessie—there—it—comes—Oh, God! how exquisite!"

Our delicious feeling was ravishing after I

shot a long charge of creamy spend into the hungry depths of Tessie's cunnie.

She quickly jumped off the bed and let the stuff escape in a morning pee. Returning to the bed we all had a nap. At six o'clock we all arose and went our way. Tessie remarked: "Oh, Gus, I never had such a treat in all my life. Madge picked a star performer when she picked you."